STARFIRE AT TRAITOR'S GATE

by C. Westhead

PublishAmerica
Baltimore

© 2006 by C. Westhead.
All rights reserved. No part of this book may be reproduced, stored in a retrieval system or transmitted in any form or by any means without the prior written permission of the publishers, except by a reviewer who may quote brief passages in a review to be printed in a newspaper, magazine or journal.

First printing

All characters appearing in this work are fictitious. Any resemblance to real persons, living or dead, is purely coincidental.

At the specific preference of the author, PublishAmerica allowed this work to remain exactly as the author intended, verbatim, without editorial input.

ISBN: 1-4241-3060-3
PUBLISHED BY PUBLISHAMERICA, LLLP
www.publishamerica.com
Baltimore

Printed in the United States of America

For Allan

CHAPTER 1

"They should be in contact by now." Lieutenant Starfire Tehr glanced at the wall clock in flight control for the tenth time in as many minutes. She knew better than to disturb the flight technicians, one of whom was desperately trying to contact Flight One Seven. Starfire's heart leapt when she heard Nik's voice, almost drowned out by static.

"We hear you strength one, Flight One Seven. Say again." The tech at the desk looked ridiculously young to Starfire who had reached the grand old age of twenty-two herself, but she resisted the urge to push the young man aside and take control. The grating sound of static filled the room again and Starfire, along with the two technicians, unconsciously leaned forward, as if being nearer to the speakers would help them pick up the fading traces of speech. The young flight controller, whose I.D. badge labelled him as 'Ensign Blik', danced his fingers over the glass controls on his console as he tried to filter out the noise. The static lessened slightly and Starfire picked out the sound of engines under stress.

"They're in trouble," she gritted and Ensign Blik glanced away from his console long enough to glare her into silence. By rights, she should not have been there but both techs knew her connection to the Flight Commander and they were too busy to try and make her leave.

"Flight One Seven, I can't hear you, but perhaps you can hear me. If you can, switch off your communicator twice. The static cleared and silence descended. It came on again, then off then on. Starfire and Blik exchanged grins. It wasn't much but it was communication.

"Very good, Commander Nikal. We'll use the standard 'one' for yes and 'two' for no. Do you understand?" There was silence, then static. "Good, Commander. Is your pilot conscious?" Two bursts of static made Starfire bite her lip. Nik was an average pilot at best. Not a bonus in a damaged fighter coming in hot for an emergency landing. "I understand, Commander. Can you eject the pilot section?" Another two bursts of static. "Can you shut down your engines?" Another negative. "All right, Commander, engage auto pilot and we'll bring you in from here."

Ensign Blik threw the other tech a quick look. She shook her head. "Sorry Commander, auto will not engage and we can't shut your engines down for a rescue in space. Can you eject your fuel? Okay don't worry, stand by for a grab, we'll tow you in." Four busts of static greeted this and Starfire leaned towards Blik to mutter something into his ear. His initial glare of annoyance turned to understanding and he continued in a calm voice, "Commander, are your engines on overheat? Right, we'll have to get you in asap. I'll talk you through it; just do everything I say. Do you understand?"

There was one burst of static and Ensign Blik continued in a calm voice. "Okay Commander, we have access to your on-board systems so please listen carefully. Channel all your remaining power into your port engine and cross patch your stabilisers into the port braking system. Good, that's a little better. You are two thousand K's out and closing on course. There's a fire in the port fuel cell. Put it out. Good. Your landing thrusters are inoperative so you'll have to glide in. Use runway 10 on the surface. Do you have a lock?" The comlink switched off, then on. "All emergency systems are online down here. Good luck, Commander. We'll see you in five."

"You'll make it, Nik," whispered Starfire under her breath. A long moment passed and she began to feel hopeful, then a dull rumble shook the room and most of the lights on Ensign Blik's console flashed red. They stared at each other in horror for a split second then Starfire was making for the aircar at a sprint.

Once inside, she fumed at the delay as the little shuttle sped upwards along a maze of tunnels, stopping at junctions to let through cars with a higher priority. She sat with her head in her hands, fearing the worst. The flight control room was five floors down. If they had felt the impact there, the crash must have been severe. The aircar stopped and the doors slid silently open. Starfire rushed out and pushed her way through a throng of people who were all pressed against the glass of massive, wall sized windows, jostling to get a better view of the organised chaos as the rescue teams tried to salvage what was left of Flight One Seven.

It was a beautiful morning of blue and gold on Planet Terrell, a stark contrast to the concrete runway and grey, metal surface buildings. A pall of black smoke still hung in the air and a blanket of foam covered the runway. Starfire's experienced eye could see that the fighter's glide path had been too steep and too fast. The fighter's nose had hit the runway and it had cart wheeled end over end to skid into the netting and eventually slide to a halt on its back, crushing the pilot section. As foam slid gently over the polished hull, the scorch marks of laser fire could be seen on its port side, explaining the port engine failure. A hover crane appeared, lowered magnetic clamps to the underside of the wreck and raised it slowly from the ground. One of the rescue crew ran forward to peer up into the tangled mass of metal. He shook his head slowly, spoke into his comlink, made a cutthroat gesture and waved the waiting ambulance away.

"Come on Lieutenant, there's nothing you can do here." Starfire jumped as a quiet voice invaded her thoughts. She turned her head to see a tall Aurian Captain standing next to her. He placed his hand on her upper arm and she realised that she had been clutching a guardrail so tightly that her knuckles were white. "My name's Raan." He stuck out his hand in an awkward attempt at a Terrellian greeting gesture. "I knew Nik."

"He spoke of you," answered Starfire, taking the offered hand and deciding not to mention that most of what Nik said had not been complimentary.

"I'm sure he did," muttered Raan dryly. "Come on, let's get out of here." He guided her into a vacant aircar and quickly programmed in their destination. Once they were moving, he took a deep breath and blurted, "Look Lieutenant, about you and Nik…"

"He told me you didn't think I should have been his pilot," blurted Starfire, "but it was Nik's decision."

"Yeah, I know," he gritted, clearly not in agreement with Nik's choice.

"Look, just because I'm a 'Terry', it doesn't mean I can't fly, Captain." Starfire raised her voice slightly, "I have a Pilot Five classification and I worked damned hard to get it."

"I know how good a pilot you are, Lieutenant."

Then what is it? Sir." She added the title as an afterthought.

"You held him back." Raan clenched his fists in anger. "He would have been a Colonel by now if he didn't have a 'Terry' for a sidekick. He was a good man."

"Do you think I don't know that?" Starfire looked up at him, suppressing her anger. "I tried to get transferred but he wouldn't hear of it." Raan looked quickly away and made a visible effort gain control of his emotions. When he looked back at Starfire, he could see the anguish in her eyes and cursed himself for being all kinds of a fool.

"Damn it, I'm sorry, Lieutenant," he began softly, "I shouldn't have said that, I spoke out of line." He raised his hand to touch hers but Starfire batted it away and they sat facing in each other in stony silence. She suddenly realised that Nik had been her only friend and now she was truly alone. A large tear of self pity slid down her cheek and she hastily brushed it aside, not wanting to let the Captain see she had been crying.

The aircar stopped at a junction and the panel lit up to show three minutes waiting time unless they had higher priority. Raan entered a higher code and it started moving again, going around the other waiting cars.

"Neat trick," grunted Starfire.

"I don't like to use if too often," answered Raan. "It's a master code and has top priority and privacy clearance. I kind of acquired it." He threw Starfire a cheeky grin and the hard lines left his face. He looked much younger when he smiled and the colour had come back into his face. Auria, Raan's home planet, had a red sun and all Aurians had the same distinctive honey coloured skin, chestnut red hair and amber eyes.

The aircar swerved suddenly and Starfire almost fell off her perch, hastily grabbing the seat strap. Raan winked at her and Starfire could see that the descriptions applied to Raan by Commander Nikal had every possibility of being true. He was a gambler of considerable note and had supposedly bedded every available female in the sector. Starfire had to admit that he was a fine looking man, possessing a perfectly proportioned body that looked lithe and supple under the grey Captain's uniform. It was topped with a fine head possessing classically handsome features and a smile that would melt a miser's heart. A standard Marine issue blaster hung low at his right side and Starfire could see that the holster flap was cut away to allow easier access to the weapon.

Raan was using his own system to appraise Starfire and worked from the feet up. He saw knee length boots, into which were tucked the legs of a flying suit that would have been regulation had it not been a size too small. A standard issue hand laser was clipped to her belt and she wore the insignia of an Aurian Marine Lieutenant on her left breast. Chin length, curly brown hair framed a pretty face and eyes that were a strange combination of brown and green, something that he believed Terrellians called 'hazel'. Although Starfire's skin had seen exposure to the outside and her face had tanned slightly, she still looked unnaturally pale to Raan. The aircar slowed and the light over the entrance door changed from red to amber.

"We're here," announced Raan pointlessly.

"Where is here?" asked Starfire, rising from her seat.

"The freighter that Nik and his pilot were riding shotgun on is due to dock. Word has it that the General's son flew it in."

"Must have had something important on board," mused Starfire.

"Replacement troops," began Raan. "These pirate raids are getting worse by the week. It's bad enough being posted to this god forsaken hole in the ground but to have to play nursemaid to a bunch of 'Terrys'...." He tailed off.

"Don't worry about it, Captain," said Starfire, dryly. "And just for the record, I was born here and I think it's a miserable hole in the ground as well."

"Anyway," Raan studied the aircar instrument panel at great length to cover up his embarrassment, "Let's go see what Nik gave his life to protect." The panel light changed from amber to green and the doors slid open to reveal a viewing balcony, running thirty feet above the floor of a massive circular silo. Raan used his illicit code to keep the aircar waiting and they walked to the edge, leaned over the railing and looked upwards toward the open sky fifty stories above them. The silo was ringed with apartments and most of their private balconies were occupied with Aurians; mainly in uniform, but there were a few off duty Marines as well. The sound of engines grew to a crescendo and the sky darkened as a gigantic ship appeared over the silo's edge. The freighter began to sink slowly, the noise from its downward thrusters negated by mufflers in the silo walls. Starfire and Raan watched as the ship dropped past them and their eyes met as they surveyed the damage it had sustained. Her turret guns had been obliterated and scorch marks covered her hull. Two of her five rear thrusters were blackened and smoking and as the ship landed on creaking hydraulic legs, automatic systems cut in and covered the stern with foam.

Even a few of the normally space shy Terrellians watched from behind glass for a brief look at the huge metal galleon as it squatted hissing steam and exhaust gasses on the launch silo floor. Terrellians lived far beneath their planet in subterranean cities, built after a long forgotten disaster forced them from the surface. They were a race of agoraphobics and were treated with disdain by most of the other races. Their skill in mining and terra-forming, gained after the destruction of their planet's surface, was their main export and they had reluctantly allowed The Aurian Space Marines to build a base in their upper levels and operate a small space port which they used as a trading station. To see an off world Terrellian was rare and a Terrellian Marine even more so but Starfire ignored the stares and points of a few Aurians as she and Raan leaned out over their balcony for a better view. The passenger ramps lowered and frightened people started to stream from the exits. They were businessmen and traders mostly; greeting their Terrellian counterparts like long lost friends, their prejudices forgotten in their haste for profit.

Starfire took in the busy scene as hover trolleys zoomed from the cargo holds, carrying cases and crates with baggage handlers bustling behind them. A line had formed at the check in desks and a few excited Aurian children, probably from the families of the replacement troops, chased each other up and down the queues. The air smelled of cold dampness and aviation fuel and Starfire risked a glance upward, pleased that the silo roof had slid into place. She had been away from Terrell since she was a child, but the open air still un-nerved her if she didn't prepare herself for it.

"Come on Lieutenant, let's go down," said Raan, turning from the railing. They entered the aircar and he programmed it for the short ride. The doors opened straight out onto the silo floor and Raan nodded briefly to one of the marines on duty, who grinned at him and waved them through. He steered

Starfire through the crowds to the aft cargo bay of the gigantic ship. Switchgear hummed loudly and the huge door began to drop down, making a ramp for those inside to descend.

The first to exit was a group of Marines. They didn't look too happy to be arriving on Terrell, but at least they were alive. It wasn't much fun being in the cargo hold of a ship under fire as both Raan and Starfire could testify. It didn't seem to have affected the Troop Commander, who spotted Raan, gave him a broad smile and marched towards him, hand outstretched. He shouldered past Starfire as if she didn't exist but she was used to that and stood back to let him pass.

"Raan," he beamed, "What are you doing on this doomed rock? I thought you were on a month's leave."

"I was Sir, but I've been recalled."

"Too bad, kid. Hey, that was some ride. I thought we'd bought it." He lit up a black cheroot, oblivious to the potential fire hazard and ignoring all the prohibitive signs. "Do you know who was riding shotgun? I was up on deck and saw him get hit pretty hard. If he got back, I'd like to shake his hand."

"It was Nik," answered Raan quietly. "He didn't make it."

"Hell, I'm sorry Raan. Give my condolences to your folks. If it's any consolation at all, he got us through. I don't think we'd have made it if he hadn't drawn their fire."

"Thank you Sir." The Commander clapped Raan on his shoulder and walked away. Starfire stared at Raan and raised one eyebrow, her expression asking the question. "He was my brother," said Raan quietly.

"I didn't know, gasped Starfire. "He never told me."

"Well, I guess he wouldn't at that." Raan looked down at his boots. "We never saw eye to eye. We had an argument the last time I saw him on Tragon 3." Starfire touched his arm gently but

Raan shrugged it away. "I don't need any sympathy from you, Lieutenant."

"And I wasn't giving you any," she answered, hotly. "I need all my sympathy for myself." She spun round, head held high, and meant to stalk off in a dramatic exit but collided with a tall, grey haired Marine, who stood in her path. "Get out of my way, damn it," she snapped and then realised that she had tried to elbow a full General aside.

"Lieutenant Starfire, Captain Raan," he said quietly, "I'm glad you two have finally met." His expression softened "I wish to offer my condolences to you both. Captain Nikal was a fine Marine. He will be missed."

"General, do you know why I was grounded?" Starfire glared up at General Dubois, Commander in Chief of the Aurian Base on Terrell. "If I had been with Nik I could have brought it in. I could have!" She had raised her voice and people were beginning to stare. Starfire slowly released the front of Dubois' jacket, stepped back and saluted. "I'm sorry, Sir," she babbled, face turning scarlet. "I don't know what came over me."

The General raised his hand for silence, straightening his rumpled grey jacket where Starfire had grasped both sides of it in her urgency and regained his dignified posture.

"I will explain everything to you later," he stated calmly. "First, I want you to do something for me." He raised his head as if scanning the crowd and then nodded in satisfaction. "Ah, do you see that man there?"

One man stood out from the descending passengers. He was tall, dressed in black and walked with proud grace, clearing the way for a large, pompous Aurian to follow him. This Aurian was extremely well dressed in heavy, embroidered silks and was followed in turn by a trio of chattering sycophantic servants who orbited him like asteroids around a small moon. One of the other passengers, a young med tech if his white tunic was anything to go by, inadvertently strayed into the fat Aurian's path. Instantly the tall man put himself between them, his eyes cold and hard and the young man side stepped with a gulp. The fat Aurian beamed and waddled onwards, the tall man keeping pace at his side like a lean, tamed wolf. He seemed to stiffen, his hand resting gently on a huge blaster that hung low on his hip. He slowed his pace and scanned the crowds with narrowed gaze as if he knew that Raan and Starfire were watching him. He seemed totally unaware that he was the centre of attention and continued on his way, guiding the Aurian towards a group of merchants who were clearly waiting for them in the V.I.P. section. He was a gunman, a hired bodyguard and he was Terrellian.

"Well now I've seen everything," muttered Raan. They had turned away as soon as they realised the gunman knew he was being watched and headed for the nearest aircar stage.

"I'm not the only Terrellian offworlder you know." snapped Starfire.

"Oh, yeah," put in Raan. "Out of a planet of maybe 25 billion, there must be all of a hundred of you."

"That is why I need you to find that man," put in General Dubois.

"The 'Terry'?" asked Raan.

"His name is Hal, Captain. I want you to find him, hire him and bring him to my quarters at oh eight hundred tonight."

CHAPTER 2

The big yellow sun was slowly setting as Starfire and Raan walked out onto the surface of Terrell. The rocky landscape was barren of plant life and a hot, dry wind stirred pale sand around their boots as they walked. The aircar had brought them out onto the other side of the city, away from the Aurian Base. The only visible signs of planet habitation were ventilation shafts, communication masts and a few maintenance ports. Starfire was about to point out to Raan that if they were found out here they would be in serious trouble with the Terrellian Council and probably court martialled, but then she saw the way he scanned the rocks. He must have known the risk they were taking but he said in a pleasant tone,

"Terrell has breathtaking scenery don't you think?"

"It's a wasteland and you know it," she smiled grimly. "You're speaking of my homeland you know, I could get a little touchy." They grinned at one another then were both instantly alert as the sound of furtive movement reached their ears.

"Is that you Cap?" called a whining voice. Raan stepped out from the rock they had dived behind and answered,

"It's all right Cully. It's just me and a friend, you can come out."

"She's a 'Terry', Cap." The voice had a wheedling tone that Starfire found increasingly irritating, but she'd had far worse receptions from Aurians. The little man stepped into view and she had a chance to study him in more detail. He couldn't have been more than five feet tall and he was dressed in filthy overalls with a logo that claimed him to be a sanitation engineer, third class.

"Cully, come and meet Lieutenant Starfire," grinned Raan. The little man sniffed and brushed a grimy hand through his lank, greasy hair. He wiped his other hand down the leg of his overalls and raised it palm held upwards, Aurian style. Starfire returned the traditional 'weapons free' gesture and pasted a smile across her features, trying not to notice the smell of dirty drains and stale sweat that hung around him like a cloud.

"Any friend of Cap's is a friend of mine," he droned ingratiatingly.

"Lucky me," she answered, dryly. Cully opened is mouth to speak again but Raan spoke quickly.

"Cut the chat, Cully and get to the point," he said, motioning Starfire to keep watch. "Did you get what I wanted?"

"I found your man, Cap. He's right here in the city."

"I could have told you that," retorted Raan.

"Yeah, but I know where."

"All right, where?" sighed Raan.

"First things first, Cap. I gotta live you know." Cully sniffed again, held out his dirty hand and waited for Raan to fill it with credits. When this was done and the bounty stashed away in his overalls, Cully motioned Raan over and whispered in his ear while keeping a wary eye on Starfire.

"Right then, let's go." Raan's voice made Starfire jump as her gaze had been turned away from them towards the aircar exit.

"Where did the smelly man go?" she asked. "Did he have the information?"

"Let's get off the surface first," answered Raan, striding across the sand to the waiting aircar. Once inside, he shut the doors and programmed their destination using the information Cully had given to him. As they were no longer on the Aurian base they had to pay to use the aircar and Raan put in an extra five credits to ensure their privacy.

"Well, where are we going then?" asked Starfire.

"The guy we want is called Hal. He's riding shotgun on the big fat Aurian we saw. And get this, he's none other than Dolton Blass."

"Dolton Blass the gangster?"

"The very same. Only don't let him hear you say that. He's managed to get himself pretty high up on the High Council. They say he'll soon be Minister for Trade."

"Well I don't like the look of him," muttered Starfire under her breath.

"I'm sure he'll be all broken up about that if he ever gets to hear of it," said Raan dryly.

"So, we find this Dolton Blass guy and we find Hal."

"That's about it. They're staying at the Galaxy; got a suite on the top floor. That's where we're going now."

"You want to go into the city? In uniform?"

"Sure, why not?"

"Steel City's off limits" pointed out Starfire. "And besides that, Terrellians hate Aurians at the best of times; Marines they hate even more."

"Terrellians hate everyone," countered Raan with a wry smile. "Why ask us to come here if they didn't want us around?"

"Because of the pirate raids, nothing else," explained Starfire. "You know how they hate space flight. They don't even have any ships. How the hell could they fight a space war?"

"All right, all right, I'm sorry." Raan held up his hands in mock surrender. "They still asked for our help though," he muttered under his breath. "Damn it, we're not even allowed in their fair city but it's all right for us to go out there and die for them."

"Oh shut up!" snapped Starfire, then she caught his eye. "Shut up, Sir I mean," she added hastily. Raan smiled to show there was no ill feeling and sat down beside her as the air car travelled on.

"Look kid, I know it's none of my business, but just how did a Terrellian end up a Lieutenant in the Aurian Space Marines?"

"It's no secret," began Starfire, "I was born here in Steel City. My father was killed in an accident when I was a baby so my mother went to work for The Aurian Ambassador and his wife while they were posted here. They couldn't have children of their own and when my mother died they took me in. They were very kind to me but they were getting old and I guess I was a little wild and they couldn't handle me. They took me with them when they went back to Auria and put me in the Marine Cadets. I've been in The Marines ever since. How about you?" Raan shrugged,

"There's not much to tell. All my family are in the Marines. Nik was older than me and he went first. I wasn't that bothered about joining, but it's kind of expected of you in our family." He would have said more, but they had reached their destination. The Galaxy Hotel was so large and important that it had its own aircar stage and they stepped out onto a plush royal blue carpet in the main lobby. A hush descended on the room and all eyes turned their way. Starfire grinned at Raan.

"What's it feel like to be the odd one out, Captain?" Raan didn't reply. Used to being popular, he didn't like the hostile looks being thrown at him by every Terrellian and he began to realise what it must have like for Starfire on Auria. A few banner-waving youngsters were being hustled out of the main doors by City Police and Starfire walked over to the desk to ask the clerk what was going on.

"Well," he began eagerly, "Dolton Blass is in the top suite. He's booked for a month and paid triple rates. The manager says his money is as good as anyone else's so what the heck? Anyway, a few student types decided to protest about the Aurians coming here and taking over all the best rooms." He caught Raan's accusing eye and babbled, "Well, live at let live, that's my motto." Raan threw him a dirty look and turned towards the internal aircar.

"Welcome to the Galaxy Hotel. Which floor sir?" asked the small robot attendant. Normally a hotel aircar would have been self-programming but this was a prestige establishment. The little cigar shaped machine bore a strong resemblance to a rubbish disposer and hovered about two feet off the floor. It had a smiley clown face painted on it that someone in marketing obviously thought was happy but would have given a small child nightmares for a week. It was obvious that they were going to get nowhere until they answered it so Raan said,

"Top Suite."

"Thank you madam," it replied and the little car shot straight upwards for twenty seconds and then stopped. The doors whooshed open and the machine droned, "Top Suite Madam."

"Thank you," said Starfire on her way out.

"You're welcome Sir."

"Oh come on." Raan pulled her through the doors, "Don't encourage it." They found themselves in a richly carpeted square hall. Directly opposite them were large double doors and another robot rose off its stand to greet them as they approached. It looked like a rubbish disposer too, but there was no smiley face and it was sprayed gold to match ornate baroque decor.

"We'd like to see…." began Raan

"Mr Blass has given strict instructions that he is not to be disturbed." It cut in with a sing song, tinny voice.

"We haven't come to see Mr Blass," Starfire tried, "We've would like to see…"

"Mr Blass has given strict instructions that he is not to be disturbed." Raan gave a weary sigh, grabbed the machine and shoved it aside. It hummed across the hall, cannoned off the opposite wall, bumped into a bronze statue of a naked cherub and address it with a voice that had risen an octave. "Mr Blass has given strict instructions…" Raan kicked it savagely as he walked by and silence descended. They both studied the high ornate doors and Starfire pressed the vid button. There was no answer so she tried again. There was still no answer.

"They must be out," stated Raan

"Maybe they just don't want to see anyone," put in Starfire.

"No, there's nobody at home. Leave this to me," stated Raan in a businesslike tone. He pulled a small toolkit from his tunic pocket and gently removed the panel covering the automatic door controls. He probed with a long, thin instrument into the mass of circuitry and pressed the panel number display. He worked with speed and dexterity and finally stepped back with a satisfied grunt.

"That should do it." The doors slid apart about three feet and Starfire silently applauded. Raan bowed from the waist in acknowledgment and stayed bent double as the barrel of an extremely large pistol appeared from the other side of the gap and came to rest on the tip of his nose. The gun moved back a little and motioned them inside. They walked in a little sheepishly and Starfire, deciding that attack was the best form of defence blurted out,

"We did knock!" as if that excused breaking and entering. The owner of the gun was the tall Terrellian they had seen earlier in the cargo bay. He was still dressed in black, which made his colouring look even more pale to Raan's eyes. His hair was wispy and fair and his dark grey eyes were faintly mocking as he said softly,

"Didn't you know that…"

"Yeah, Mr Blass has given strict instructions that he is not to be disturbed," cut in Raan dryly. He did not like being made a fool of, particularly by a Terrellian—even one as menacing as this. The blaster was now pointing down at the carpet but it was held in an easy, negligent grip that gave the impression it could very quickly be raised to heart height if required.

"It isn't Mr Blass we've come to see," began Starfire.

"Then it is my loss, my dear." said an oily voice. An obese Aurian appeared from a side door and waved Hal aside. "Sit down and introduce yourselves. I was most amused by your attempts to break into my rooms. The least I can do is hear what you have to say before I have you arrested."

"Our business is with him," Raan motioned his head towards Hal, not liking the Aurian's tone. To his further annoyance, Blass laughed out loud. His piggy head bobbed up and down and his chins wobbled. Perspiration beaded his face and neck at which he dabbed with a scented kerchief in a vain effort to stem the odious flow.

"Really," began Starfire. "We have come to see Mr Hal."

"My dear girl," Blass leered at Starfire in what he obviously considered to be a winning smile, "Hal is my protection. He is bought and paid for. What ever it is you came to say, you will say in front of me."

"We came to hire Mr Hal." said Starfire firmly. Once again Dolton Blass started to laugh, wiped his face with another kerchief and dropped the soiled one onto the floor without watching it fall.

"I've already told you, Hal belongs to me until his contract ends. He is not available for work. Goodbye."

"Now just wait a minute...." snarled Raan. He stepped towards the fat man but was brought up short by Hal's pistol, which was now aimed at his chest in an unwavering grip. Blass snapped his podgy fingers and motioned Hal forward without looking at him. Hal lowered the gun slightly and spoke in a quiet, offworlder drawl.

"It's like the man says, I'm not for hire." Starfire tried to drag up a winning smile for Blass.

"Isn't there way you'll let him go? Our commanding officer has empowered us to offer any sum you would care to name."

"I won't release Hal from his contract at any price. He's my protection. I need him."

"So does General Dubois," countered Starfire.

"Dubois?" cut in Hal, eyes narrowed and showing emotion for the first time. "Dorian Dubois?" Starfire and Raan exchanged a glance. While they knew the General must have a first name, neither of them knew what it might be."

"Sure," lied Raan. "That's his name all right."

"Dolton, I owe this man a life debt," began Hal quietly. "I must honour it."

"I've paid your fee. You will stay and protect me. Now do as I say and throw these people out."

"You can have your fifty thousand back," stated Hal flatly. "With interest. I know a good man who'll do the job."

"I don't want another man, Hal. I want the best and you're it." Blass started to whine like a petulant child. "My life is under constant threat and I need you here." His expression hardened and he raised his voice and snarled menacingly," If you walk out on me I'll make sure you never work in this sector again." An uncomfortable silence filled the room and Raan coughed.

"Well er, look, if Mr Blass changes his mind, you'll find us in the Marine Quarter, Officer's lounge, Level Eight."

"I won't," yelped Blass. "Now get out before I call security." It was clear Hal wasn't going to say anything else so Starfire and Raan looked each other and walked out of the apartment.

"What do we do now?" asked Raan as they sat in the aircar on their way back to the base. "The General won't be too happy about this." Starfire shrugged.

"We tried our best. The man just isn't available. You'll just have to tell the General."

"Now wait just a minute, he asked us both to find him."

"He gave you the message, Captain. And you're the senior officer."

"Don't you try that rank thing on me, Lieutenant, it won't work." They were still arguing about it as they stepped out of the aircar into the Officer's lounge. It went quiet and every face turned their way. Raan hissed into Starfire's ear, "What the hell is everyone looking at?"

"Me," answered Starfire, "With you." One of the younger

Ensigns, a little the worse for drink, leaned across the table and said in a stage whisper to his drinking partners,

"Commander Nikal isn't even cold yet and she's got herself in with another...." which was as far as he got, that being the length of time it took Raan to charge across the room and grab the startled young man by his jacket. Cards and drinks went flying as Raan hauled the boy out of his seat and bunched a fist under his nose.

"Now you apologise to the Lieutenant, you little crud or I'll knock your head off your shoulders." Another of the youths reached for Raan, meaning to spin him around, but Starfire got there first. A swift punch sent him careering backwards towards another two young men, who were just rising out of their seats. All three of them went down in a tangled heap and Raan threw the first young man on top of them in disgust. "Does this happen often?" he asked Starfire as they walked away.

"All the time, Captain. I'm used to it." They made their way to the bar, ignoring the cold stares from most of the younger troopers. Time passed and there was still no sign of Hal. Raan looked at his wrist com-link for the twentieth time. It showed 19:45. He finished his drink, stood up and sighed.

"It looks like this Hal guy isn't going to show. Somebody has to tell the old man; I guess it might as well be me." When Starfire showed no sign of weakening, he glared at her and strode to the aircar with Starfire rushing to keep pace at his side.

They hesitated outside the door of the General's private quarters then Raan pressed the vid button and stepped back. The General's face appeared on the tiny screen and he smiled warmly.

"Ah, Captain Raan, Lieutenant Starfire, please come in." The door opened with a hiss and they walked inside. It was tastefully furnished in different shades of oatmeal and the General rose from a much used beige chair to greet them. He poured out two drinks and walked towards them, hands outstretched. He looked so pleased to see them that Starfire couldn't bear it and blurted out,

"Sir," she began, "Hal..." but the words stuck in her throat. Raan decided to bail her out.

"Hal couldn't come, General," he finished, trying to look sorry. The General gazed past them as a sardonic voice from the door said,

"I wouldn't say that." They spun round to see the Terrellian gunman lounging against the doorway, arms folded.

"Come in, Hal, come in," beamed Dubois, handing him Raan's drink. "I knew you wouldn't let me down."

CHAPTER 3

Hal walked past Starfire and Raan to shake the General's hand and accept a black cheroot, which he lit without haste.

"Now," smiled Dubois, "I would like you to meet two other people before I explain why I have asked you here. If you would follow me please." He led the way through a connecting door into a small dining room. It contained a circular table and six chairs, two of which were occupied. A tall, athletic looking Aurian man stood up with military precision and Raan exchanged a glance with Starfire. This must be the General's son. He had handsome features and was dressed in the uniform of a Major in the Space Marines.

"Please meet Del," began the General. After Aurian greetings had been made and reciprocated, he motioned to the young woman who lounged in the chair next to him with a bored expression on her face. "And this is Erion." The woman, who made no effort to rise, had a slender body and would have been very pretty if she hadn't been wearing too much make up. She wore skimpy, cheap civilian clothes and her wrists and neck sparkled with garish jewellery. Raan, who considered himself the expert in these matters, had her pegged as an entertainer of some sort. She wore her thick, chestnut hair in a short wedge cut and had it combed forward, off worlder style, so that it reached a point just above her regal nose. She raised one finger in greeting as if this was a tremendous effort and then looked away. The General motioned for them to be seated around the table.

"You may say what you wish here, off the record and in complete secrecy. My quarters have been checked for listening devises." A cigar shaped robot floated in carrying a steaming plate of food in each of it's four spindly metal arms. It placed meals in front of everyone and drew back to alight on a podium in the corner of the room. Starfire and Raan looked at the fresh food on their plates and grinned at each other. Their palettes were more used to Marine rations and reconstituted fare, but this looked like the real thing and they tucked in with a barely concealed relish.

"I'd like to start by putting everyone in the picture here." General Dubois waited until they had all finished eating and coffee had been served. "As you know, Terrell has a sister planet orbiting this sun. It is called Serrell and is known to be uninhabited. What you probably won't know, is that a little over two hundred years ago, a party of settlers was sent to colonise Serrell."

There were a few surprised glances over the table at this remark. Terrellians were known to distrust any form of outside travel and considered going out on to the surface a feat reserved for the incredibly brave or insane. After a prolonged and bitter civil war, there had been nothing left on the planet's surface but rubble and radiation. The survivors who had made it underground, stayed there and gradually a culture grew. People began to extend their caves, joining them with tunnels until a vast network of concrete and steel thrived under the surface. When the contamination had gone, the cities were so well established that no one bothered to leave their safe environment. It was controlled and easy to protect and the Council of the Electorate did all it could to discourage trips out into the open. It eventually led to a whole planet of pale skinned, agoraphobic people, totally reliant on trade for its existence. A cosy, repressed atmosphere and fierce patriotism had been encouraged and maintained by the Electorate, and few Terrellians ever left their home world. Those that did were considered outcasts at best or traitors at worst.

"How did they get anyone to volunteer for that?" asked Starfire.

"It was the Science Council that decided that life on the surface of Serrell might be possible and they pushed a motion through the Senate for an expedition. The Electorate were against it from the start, but this was at the time of the great 'flu epidemic and public opinion was wavering." The General took a sip of coffee and continued, "Apart from the scientists, most of the colonists were anti-Electorate and mal contents. A few were plain adventurers or people the Electorate wanted out of the way. At any rate, they preferred to take their chances on Serrell rather than spend their lives in the rehabilitation units." Dubois caught Hal's eye at this point and the gunman met his gaze without flinching. Hal could testify to the uselessness of rehabilitation, Terrellian style. In his case it had the opposite effect and he burst forth on an unsuspecting universe like a rogue comet. He had stowed away on Dubois' shuttle and the

Captain, as he was then, had helped the young tearaway escape. "Anyway," continued Dubois, "Nobody quite knows what went wrong, but six months later, there was a massive nuclear explosion on the surface of Serrell."

"It's in our history books," broke in Starfire, looking across at Hal, who nodded his agreement. "At the time, it caused chaos here. We were told it was some sort of axial tilt in Serrell's orbit or something, certainly not a nuclear explosion."

"Yes, Lieutenant," said Dubois, "In a way, it served the council well, for if there had been any installations on the surface of Terrell at that time, they would have been totally destroyed. It made their case for staying underground that much stronger." He paused for another sip of coffee and his robot passed him a cigar, which he lit and savoured. Raan poured out some wine and threw the Aurian woman a broad smile and a wink. She smiled back but offered no further encouragement. Starfire kicked him under the table as the General continued. "By the time and Aurian rescue team was called in, they found only heavy contamination and no sign of life. It was assumed everyone had perished and no other attempts were made to go to Serrell again."

"Until?" prompted Raan.

"Until six months ago when, through diplomatic channels, Serrell declared war on Terrell and the first attacks began."

"So they aren't pirate raids," exclaimed Starfire.

"No Lieutenant, The Council of the Electorate used the pirate story to stop widespread panic among the population. The attacks are real, as you can testify and they have almost choked off the shipping routes. That is why we set up a military base here a few months ago. Serrell is heavily shielded and we cannot scan it to find out what is going on."

"Can't you blast the shield?" asked Raan.

"The Electorate will not allow us to do that." He took time out to re-light his cigar and take a few puffs. "They say that Serrell is under their jurisdiction and any attack upon it would constitute an act of war on Terrell also. They are treating this as an internal matter and they are trying to open diplomatic channels."

"With respect, that sucks, Sir," put in Raan.

"Something is far from right and that's a fact, Captain," began the General. "Politics is going on here, I think. I have tried to find out more but I have drawn a blank." He looked at them all in turn, "What I want is a small strike team to land on Serrell, find out what is going on and stop these attacks."

"Just like that?" murmured Hal.

"Just like that," confirmed Dubois. He gave his empty coffee mug to the robot and accepted a glass of wine. "The Serrellians must be getting outside help from somewhere. The weaponry they are using is extremely advanced."

"Why not just blast them from space?" asked Raan. "Once it's done and the war's over the Council will have to agree with you."

"If only it were that simple, Captain," he answered. "As I have said, the planet is heavily shielded. We could not get near enough to send the bombers in even if we did have clearance from Terrell."

"If the Bombers can't get near," began Starfire, "how do you expect a strike team get through?"

"Yeah," began Raan. "They're hardly going to let a Marine strike force through the front door like they're coming to tea are they?" Dubois threw Raan a dark look.

"If you will let me continue, Captain, our logic computers

have come up with a way to penetrate their defences. I will tell you about it in more detail, then I will ask you to volunteer." They paused at this point for the robot to clear their plates away and Dubois suggested they retire to the lounge. When they were all seated, he continued. "Now, as our esteemed Captain," he motioned with his cigar, "Raan has pointed out, the enemy will not welcome Marines with open arms. They just might fall over themselves with gratitude if a party of outlaws from Terrell ask for asylum. Starfire and Hal exchanged looks, so that was why their Terrellian presence was so important. "We have shielded this planet now, so the enemy cannot know what is going on here. Unless their spies have infiltrated Aurian High Command here, which I doubt, you would be their only source of recent information. But I must warn you," began Dubois, "That if you accept this mission, there will be no chance of any help from us at all. In fact, only I and the Admiral of the Fleet will know your true purpose. Your personnel files will be altered to confirm facts about your new pasts should you accept this mission." He turned to the striking Aurian in the white suit. Neither he nor the woman had spoken during the meal and General Dubois had not made any attempt to explain their presence. The woman had steadfastly refused to accede to Raan's charm and the man had stared intently at the General throughout the meal, as if waiting for this signal.

"This is where Del and Erion will play their parts." The woman stood up and ignored a wink and a suggestive leer from Raan. She smiled at the General, who gazed at her with pride. "I did not mention earlier that Erion is my daughter and a Major in the Aurian Space Marines." Raan's mouth dropped open, and Starfire, who had guessed that there was far more to the girl than met the eye, said nothing but looked down to hide her smile.

Hal's face showed blank indifference as usual.

"Del here will masquerade as my son. Everyone has been expecting Major Dubois to be a man, so they won't be disappointed. My daughter arrived on the freighter as an ordinary civilian passenger. Her identicard lists her as a dancer called Erion Dune. For the past three months she has been plying her trade in the inns and taverns of the mining planets of the western sectors and she has managed to build up quite a reputation for herself. She wished to stay in costume, as it were, to test her disguise at close quarters." The General looked pointedly towards Raan, a twinkle in his eyes. "I think we can safely assume that she passed muster, Captain?" Raan nodded his head vigorously and Dubois continued. "Del was sent to one of these planets in the guise of my son and allowed himself to be wooed and won by Erion. I have let it be known that I have pulled strings to get my son posted here to save him from her clutches."

All eyes studied Erion in a new light. She must have been made of pretty stern stuff to carry off something like that even though she looked the part. Starfire at least, realised what it must have been like for her and Erion rose up a notch in her estimation.

"Now," said the General, "Erion is going to have a violent quarrel with my 'son' and shoot him dead. That will make her wanted for murder. Captain Raan, as of now, you are an old flame of Erion's and when she asks you for help, you will not refuse. Just in case any checks are made, and I'm sure there will be, the personnel computers have already been altered to confirm this."

"So much for volunteering," whispered Raan to Starfire out of the side of his mouth.

"Captain Raan," barked Dubois, "It was not until after a lot of thought that I had to agree with the combat computers about their choice for co pilot on this mission. I thought you far too unpredictable for the job. I would have preferred a steadier man, but it would not have looked right for a good officer to desert his post. However, if you do not wish to join us, please say so now." Raan's cheeks reddened and he shook his head. General Dubois turned his attention to Starfire.

"Lieutenant," his voice softened, "You are the only Terrellian in the Marines who can fly the freighter we have chosen for your escape. That is why I could not risk you in combat this morning. We must try to make this look as believable as possible for you all to stand any chance of success. The more Terrellians there are along, the better it will look."

"I'll go, Sir," she answered, realising there would be nowhere to call home for her after this; she would be branded a traitor from all sides.

"Well done, Starfire," said Dubois, "You will allow yourself to be persuaded to take Raan and Erion off the planet." He turned to Hal and smiled warmly. Raan thought he must see something in the steely eyed Terrellian that they had all missed. "We go back a long way, Hal, and I don't know of another man in the galaxy who has such a mastery of weapons. I know you have no political views, and I would not call upon you to repay the debt you think you owe me, so I will pay your fee myself." He leaned forward to whisper, although the room was thoroughly checked for listening devices. "Admiral Nooran and I managed to get the Trade Conference dates changed so we knew you would be here with Dolton Blass. We didn't know if you would agree to go along so the computers haven't come up with anything for your escape. If you decide to go on this mission, how are we going to get you off this planet in dubious circumstances? I know you are not a wanted man here."

"I think I am now, sir," Starfire eye's opened wide for Hal spoke with a deference that she suspected was reserved for very few people. He rose from his seat and walked over to the vidcom planted flush in the wall. The General nodded his assent and Hal turned it on, flicking through the channels until he found the one he wanted. The screen filled to show a serious faced woman, shuffling papers behind a desk. A large clock and a stylised map of Steel City were on a screen lit up behind her and these vanished to show the main lobby of the Galaxy Hotel. Police were holding back the crowds and as they waited, two men accompanied a blanket covered shape on a hover stretcher to a waiting private ambulance. The woman had a pleasant speaking voice and Hal turned up the volume so they could appreciate it to the fullest.

".... at the Galaxy Hotel this afternoon when the body of the famous Aurian tycoon Dolton Blass was found under a pile of Valasian gold pieces amounting to exactly fifty thousand credits. The family of Mr Blass is offering this sum as a reward to anyone who can supply information leading to the arrest of a Terrellian gunman and outlaw called Hal. There are no pictures available of this man, but police have issued a compufit likeness. A picture flashed across the screen which looked nothing like Hal. He grinned and switched off the machine.

"Yeah, that answers that," stated Raan dryly. "What a motley little crew we'll all make."

"Have you any questions?" asked Dubois. Erion obviously knew the plan and remained silent, Starfire and Raan began speaking at once. "One at a time please. Starfire?"

"How are you going to arrange for the death of this man," she pointed to Del, "without arousing suspicion? "Blasters with a blank load and fake blood won't fool these people, you're going to have to make it look good."

"It will be, Lieutenant." The General stood up." I'll prove it to you." He pulled a small, silenced pistol from his pocket and handed it to Hal to check.

"Got a live load," he verified. The General aimed it straight at Del and pulled the trigger. A muffled report filled the room and the Aurian stiffened, his hands going to a gaping hole in his chest. Shattered ribs showed briefly and blood poured thickly through his fingers as he slowly slid to the floor to lie pale and unmoving on the oatmeal carpet. Starfire and Raan were there in an instant.

"He's dead!" she gasped, "You killed him."

"Well that was the intention," said the General.

"Sir, he's really dead," put in Raan, his fingers checking for a non existent pulse at Del's blood spattered neck. Dubois and Erion exchanged smiles and Starfire looked wildly round at Hal for a more experienced opinion, but he remained outwardly calm. She could see though, that his hand rested gently on the butt of his blaster.

"Don't worry Lieutenant," smiled Dubois. He made a sign and the sodden Aurian stood up, colour returning to his face.

"How..." began Raan

"Did you do that?" finished Starfire, amazed.

"It is logical when you understand," answered the corpse. "One cannot kill something that does not live in the first place."

"Eh?" asked Raan, puzzled.

"He must be a robot," supplied Hal.

"You are correct," answered Del.

"A robot?" began Starfire, "But they're all grey and shiny.

This one looks like a real person." She walked round him now and studied him in more detail. "Why, he's almost flawless."

"Thank you." said Del.

"You're welcome," she answered, lifting his hand to move his fingers.

"He's a Delta Ten experimental model," supplied Erion. "We're very proud of him."

"I can see why," said Starfire, twirling the unabashed android round for a back view.

"Heck of a lot of work, just to blow up," muttered Raan. Dubois looked skyward and it was left to Erion to answer.

"Once Delta Ten has been pronounced dead by a qualified doctor, my father will put his body put aboard our private launch for burial at home. They will rendezvous with us in space and Del will join us."

"When is all this scheduled to happen?" asked Hal.

"A freighter is already standing by in launch silo six," answered Dubois. "Don't be put off by its looks, it's equipped with the latest technology and weapons. Delta Ten will be shot in the same bay, so I'd like all of you in the area before oh ten hundred. I have arranged for most of the flight to be on patrol in the eastern sector, so you should be able to get away with the minimum of damage. A couple of fighters will target your engines but will only score a glancing blow. The rear of the ship has been rigged to emit smoke so it will look as though you are badly damaged and must make an emergency landing on Serrell. This is as far as the combat computers could predict so we have made no plans as such after this point."

"Great," mumbled Raan, who secretly enjoyed a good fight. "We stand a good chance of being blown away before we leave orbit."

"Your escape must not look planned," began the General, "or you will never be allowed to land on Serrell."

"We still might not," put in Starfire,

"Then you must find another way," said Dubois simply. They all turned to look at Hal, who pushed between them, placed his drink on the table, bowed to his host and walked towards the door.

"See you tomorrow," called Starfire. Hal froze for a split second, then carried on without a backward glance. Although the door slid shut silently, he managed to convey the impression it had been slammed.

"Oh, don't mind Hal," began the General. "He'll be there tomorrow, you can be sure of that."

"We'll I'm going to turn in," said Starfire. "Something tells me tomorrow is going to be a very long day."

"Or a very short one," put in Raan, taking her arm. "May I escort you to your quarters, Lieutenant? I thought we might stop by the officers lounge for a drink. Maybe talk about Nik."

"Yes Captain," she agreed quietly. "I'd like that." They said their goodbyes and left.

"Well my dear," smiled Dubois to his daughter, "What do you think of them?" She shook her head slowly.

"What a bunch of misfits, father."

"I have every faith in the combat computers," said the General. He took his daughter's arm. "I think Captain Raan had the right idea. What say you to a drink and a game of Pan?"

CHAPTER 4

Launch bay six was virtually empty when Delta Ten strolled aimlessly to the waiting freighter. He was dressed in the Uniform of a Marine Major and looked very convincing in the role. Seemingly engrossed in checking the docking mechanism of the freighter's hatch, he did not see Erion as she came up behind him. She was dressed as she had been the night before with the addition of a shaggy wig of copper hair which hung freely to her waist.

"Hello Del," she said simply, stepping forward. "Surprised to see me?"

"Erion," said Del, jumping back as if startled. "I tried to contact you on Cariss before I left."

"I'll just bet you did," she countered. A few people looked over at the little drama with mild interest and those who did not know the tale were rapidly put in the picture by those who did. The General had put out quite a story of this turbulent romance and several people were whispering frantically and pointing their way. Erion brought forward a shiny little laser pistol and lined it shakily on Del's chest. He backed away in apparent terror, but was stopped by the closed hatchway of the ship.

"Erion, don't," he cried. He was a terrible actor, but the watchers seemed fooled and the stares turned from interest to concern.

"You ruined my chances," she spat. "I threw over the mine president for you and then you walked out on me. Nobody does that; not even the General's son!" Delta Ten moved forward, arms outstretched as if to plead with her, but Erion pulled the trigger. The report seemed unusually loud in the cavernous hangar bay and a few people jumped at the sound. Delta Ten clutched his chest and crumpled. He rolled down the ramp and measured his length on the hangar floor to lie on his side in a growing pool of blood.

One of the watchers, a young girl in the green uniform of a janitor, had let curiosity get the better of her and was close enough for Erion to reach. Her hand shot out and pulled the terrified girl towards her, keeping the little pistol at her throat and shouting,

"Keep away! Everyone just keep away!" Out of the corner of her eye she could see someone go to the wall com-link and raise the alarm. All she had to do now was wait and hope everyone played their part. Her eyes scanned the crowd and sure enough, Raan and Starfire hurried into the bay to see what all the fuss was about.

"Raan!" she screamed, "Raan, you've got to help me." The crowd parted to let them through and they made quite a convincing pair as they slammed to a halt as if they could not believe their eyes.

"Erion, what the hell have you done now?" snarled Raan. He

walked slowly forward and crouched down to roll the body onto its back. A few of the watchers grimaced at the sight of Delta Ten's false insides poking up at the world. "He's dead all right." Raan stood up to face Erion. "Let the girl go, honey."

"I can't Raan," sobbed Erion, pointing to the body with her gun. "Do you know who this is? They'll string me up! You've got to help me get away."

"Just let her go and we'll talk about it," Raan tried to calm Erion down, but his tone seemed to make her worse.

"Just remember fly boy," she spat out, "I know enough about you to have you shot." Raan stiffened and looked around him to see who had heard. To the watching audience it seemed like an admission of guilt. Erion continued, loudly, "You thought I was asleep that night, but I was listening and I got it all on vid."

"Will you shut up!" hissed Raan.

"Raan, honey," Erion whined and walked towards Raan, dragging the reluctant girl with her. "You hate the Marines, you always did," she began desperately. "Come on, babe, we were good together once, we could be again."

"Be realistic, Erion. How are you gonna get away?" Erion looked around wildly and her gaze settled on the big ship towering above them. She gazed upward and said,

"We can go in this. You can fly us out in this ship."

"I can't fly this, Erion, you'd need a Pilot Five for that." His gaze settled on Starfire, who had decided she didn't want any part of this and was trying to back out of the crowd. "Where do you think you're going?" he called softly. Starfire stopped and said,

"No way, Captain. Whatever trouble you're in, I don't want any part of it. Nik was always bailing you out and I don't aim to start."

"Come on, Star, what kind of life are you going to have without Nik? You're a 'Terry' and nobody wants you here. You're a Pilot Five and not even a Captain. Honey, a Lieutenant is all you're ever going to be if you stay here. Why don't you come with us?" Starfire seemed to hesitate and the crowd held its breath.

"If you go with them," stated a firm voice, "I'll have you shot, you Terrellian traitor." General Dubois stood there, his fists were clenched and his face was lined with grief. "I'll have you all shot!"

"Too right General," shouted another voice. It was one of the men that had caused the fight in the bar the night before and his eye was still swollen where Starfire's fist had connected with it. He held a laser rifle aimed at Starfire's back and his finger was tightening on the trigger when he suddenly stiffened and paled.

"Put the gun down, nice and easy friend." Hal walked forward with the Marine's rifle dangling from his hand. "If the ship's leaving, I'd like a ride. I have to get off this planet in a hurry and I can pay my way."

"Thanks for saving my life, mister," said Starfire.

"Just protecting the Pilot Five," he answered, walking straight by her to stand with Raan and Erion.

"Well Star, are you with us or not?" asked Raan. Starfire looked at the three of them, then at the General's furious face and seemed to make up her mind.

"I'll take you," she said firmly. Hal lined his newly acquired rifle on the crowd while they walked backwards up the ramp and Raan opened the hatch.

"Wait!" called Dubois. They turned and looked down at him. "Let the young girl go and take me in her place."

"No way General," snapped Erion, "This is our insurance." She pulled the girl roughly up the ramp.

"Then let me rendezvous with you in Space. I give you my word you will not be fired upon until the Ensign and I are safely back on this base. That should give you enough time to get into hyperspace."

"Do we have your word on that General?" asked Raan,

"You have my word," confirmed the General.

"Then you have a deal," called Erion. "Now get that silo roof open or we'll blow it away ourselves." She pulled the frightened Ensign into the ship with her. "Come on girlie," she said, "Give us no trouble and you'll be all right." Erion passed the young tech to Hal, thumped the hatch release and the door slid shut.

Outside the ship, everyone's thoughts suddenly turned to getting out as quickly as possible and it didn't take long for the bay to empty. Soon there was only the General, walking slowly behind the stretcher bearers as they carried his dead 'son' away. In the freighter's crew compartment, Starfire, Raan and Erion gazed down at the pathetic scene with glee.

"Do you think they bought it?" asked Raan.

"I think we did well, considering we only had an hour to rehearse," said Erion.

"We'll find out just how good we were when we get to Serrell," said Starfire grimly. She studied her controls. "Looks like it's fuelled up and ready to roll."

"The course is laid in and plotted," put in Erion.

"Lets go then," said Starfire to Raan. The hatch opened and Hal walked in, carrying the now unconscious technician.

"If you've killed her..." snapped Erion.

"Just a little tap, Major. She tried to jam the hatch with her com link," snarled Hal. "She knew the ship wouldn't take off with an air leak. She'll have a headache when she wakes up that's all. Besides, it's better if she doesn't hear anything."

"Just don't get smart, killer," muttered Erion. "Having you along wasn't my idea at all."

"Let's discuss it later," began Starfire. Get yourselves strapped in, we're on our way." She and Raan slowly took the large freighter upwards and headed it towards the open sky.

"Orbit confirmed," stated Raan as the ship reached the top of its arc. There was the usual slight jolt as the auto gravity compensators switched on.

"Maintaining orbit," stated Starfire. She looked across at Erion. "What now?"

"We wait for my father. He won't be long."

"Craft approaching," said Hal, his eyes on the scanner.

"Keep your finger off the firing button, Hal, it'll be the General." said Erion. Starfire glanced at Raan but said nothing. Erion seemed to be riding the gun fighter a little too hard.

"It's the General alright," put it Raan. "He's asking permission to dock."

"Check if he's alone, Raan, said Erion. "We know he is, but there may be someone scanning. It would be expected of us."

"Scan negative," said Raan.

"Right, come on bounty hunter," began Erion, "and bring the girl." Hal stood up with the semi conscious tech over his shoulder like a sack of corn and followed Erion out of the hatch.

"Your Terrellian friend certainly has a way with women," smiled Raan.

"He's not my friend," began Starfire, "but I don't like the way Erion talks to him. He's not the sort of man to take it for long."

"There's not much we can do about it right now," said Raan. "Maybe when we get to know each other a little better, things will straighten out."

"I hope so, Raan, if we live that long." answered Starfire. She glanced down at the console. They've broken the link; time to go." She fired up the motors and turned the ship away from the little launch on a direct heading out of the Terrellian system. The hatch opened again and Erion, Hal and Delta Ten entered. The robot was dressed in a white one piece suit and looked immaculate and unscathed.

"You don't look too bad for a corpse." grinned Starfire. He reproached her gently,

"I am not a corpse, Lieutenant, I am an android."

"You'll get used to Del," put in Erion. "He has no sense of humour."

"Anyone who dresses like that must have one." said Raan. Delta Ten spoke from the scanning section.

"Two fighters approaching,"

"They're our bogies," said Raan, staring into his scope.

"Turn away from them please, Starfire," ordered Erion. "Make it look as if we're trying to run."

"Aye," confirmed Starfire, making the turn.

"Bolts away," confirmed Hal. "Brace for impact." There was a loud bang and the ship lurched slightly.

"These guys are good. Just a little tap on the aft engines," confirmed Raan, passing his hand over a green crystal, "Smoke canisters activated." Starfire slowed the ship slightly and tried to fly erratically, easing the freighter towards Serrell as if she had no choice in the matter.

"Listen," began Erion, "There's my father," They heard the General's voice over the comlink.

"I gave my word to these outlaws that they would not be pursued until I returned to Terrell. You will withdraw at once. They are on fire and badly damaged. They have nowhere to go, except crash on Serrell."

"They're breaking off," confirmed Raan. "So far so good."

"Planet Serrell, dead ahead," stated Raan. "I can't scan it, though. I think the shield is up."

"That doesn't sound very reassuring," began Starfire, "Do I still make course for a landing?"

"Taker her in, Lieutenant," ordered Erion.

"I would recommend haste," put in Delta Ten. "I am picking up a small body of fighters heading this way."

"I have them," snapped Raan as Starfire turned the huge ship in a graceful roll that had the autogyros straining.

"I thought the fleet was supposed to be on the other side of this sector," muttered Starfire.

"So did I," Erion bit her lip anxiously. This was not part of the plan.

"Full shields," snapped Raan, "They'll be in range in less than two minutes."

"Can we outrun them?" asked Erion.

"Not in this bucket," answered Raan without taking his eyes off the instruments in front of him. The ship rocked as it was hit from behind.

"They're in range," said Raan.

"No, really?" muttered Hal, sarcastically.

"We can't take much more of that," warned Starfire, throwing a glare at the unabashed gunman. "The aft shield just lost thirty percent."

"What the hell happened to the General's word?" asked Raan, fingers dancing over the controls.

"Not now, Captain," answered Starfire. She threw the ship sideways and the port shield blazed as a near miss skimmed off it.

"Del, take Raan's place as Co," snapped Erion. "Hal, you and

Raan man the guns, I'll navigate." They rushed to their posts as if they had been training together for years but their exhilaration melted away as she added, "Fire warning shots."

"Warning shots?" snarled Hal in disbelief.

"Yes," said Erion, curtly. "Aim to miss." The ship was hit by another jolt that nearly threw them from their seats.

"Direct hit," said Del as if he were discussing the weather. "Aft port engine; the repair computers are on line."

"We've lost the rear shield," said Starfire, worriedly. "I must turn to face them."

"We have to defend ourselves," said Hal, flatly, his narrowed eyes squinting into the firing grid. He pressed the firing stud and grimaced as his shot went deliberately wide.

"No," snapped Erion.

"But..." began Starfire.

"I'm not discussing this with a committee. Lieutenant, I said fire warning shots."

"Damn it, the ship's breaking up, I have to do something." she blurted. There was another jolt and the lights on Starfire's console flashed red. "The port engine's on fire, Major, I'm turning." The decision to mutiny was taken out of Starfire's hands as the aft scanner lit up in a flare of white light as one of the attacking ships exploded. All eyes turned to Hal.

"Damn it, killer, I said aim to miss," snapped Erion. "They're our own people."

"They're not my people," pointed out Hal, "and they're trying to blow us out of the sky. How's it going to look if we don't shoot back?" Smoke was beginning to drift about the pilot compartment and Delta Ten left his station to use a small extinguisher on the smouldering panels.

"How long till we're in range with Serrell?" asked Erion

"Too long, Major," answered Starfire. Erion thought for a moment, then said quietly,

"Do what your best at, Hal, but try to disable if you can." The gunman nodded and began to fire at the little ships. One lost a wing, but the pilot was able to eject and another received a glancing blow that knocked out its engine. Raan, who could not fire on people who might have been his friends, had to admit that the Terrellian was good.

"They're the new recruits," he said, suddenly. "They haven't got a chance."

"They can back off," snarled Hal, scoring another glancing blow to a fighter's shield and causing it to spiral away intact.

"They're Aurians," growled Raan, 'They'll fight to the death."

"Then they're stupid," answered Hal.

"Quiet," snapped Erion, waving her hand, frantically, "It's father again."

"Who ordered this attack?" he commanded. "I have already given these people my word they would be allowed to leave."

"Sir...." a voice babbled, "I have just returned from reconnaissance and our patrol was ordered to fire on this ship."

"Who gave that order?"

"Well....... you did, Sir. The signal contained your recognition code."

"What's your name?"

"Captain Ryan, Sir."

"Well, Captain, I can assure you I gave no such order. Check my code again and break off your attack. Report to me as soon as you have landed."

"They're leaving," Raan gazed into his scope. "They're following the General."

"Phew!" sighed Erion. "Starfire, can we make it to Serrell?" Starfire shrugged.

"Maybe, Major. I don't know."

"I don't expect maybes from my crew, Lieutenant, I want answers."

"Maybe is the only answer I can give you at this time, Sir. Just let me get on with my job." Erion opened her mouth to reply then thought better of it. Starfire, who knew she was in the wrong, tried to make light of the matter and muttered under her breath, "Well, what's she going to do, have me shot?"

"Cut it Star," warned Raan and she was instantly silent.

"She has got a point though," put in Hal.

"Who asked you to butt in, killer?" snapped Erion. "We decided before we left that I was to be in command."

"You decided," corrected Hal, "I don't remember anyone asking me."

"That's what you get for missing staff meetings," put in Raan. "But let's wait until we land on Serrell before we talk it out. The crash when we hit dirt might make the question irrelevant."

"Don't be so defeatist, Captain," said Starfire. "I've never failed you yet."

"This is our first mission together," he pointed out.

"Great!" muttered Hal, Starfire threw him a grin then her expression hardened. "Better get strapped in. We're going to hit that shield soon."

"Now we'll see if my father's plan worked or not," said Erion.

"I can scan the planet now," began Raan. "The shield is down."

"Then we're safe," Erion breathed a sigh of relief.

"Don't get too complacent, Major, we've still got to land this crate," snarled Raan, leaning forward to make minute adjustments to the controls. "I think we'll be in for a bumpy ride." He glanced at Starfire, who pulled a 'who knows?' face.

"Any advance on maybe?" called Erion from behind them.

"Yeah," answered Starfire. "Maybe not."

"I thought you were supposed to be a Pilot Five." sighed Hal from the weapons section.

"Do I tell you who to kill people, bounty hunter?" asked Starfire, "No. So you let me land this thing and if I kill us all then you can criticise." Erion was amazed. She had been brought up by her father to have an open mind and did not think she was prejudiced about Terrellians. True, she had never met any before and could not work out if these two were joking or not. Aurians were on the whole, a serious lot and Erion thought she would ask Raan later. Then again, he was a little strange himself and she decided to wait and try to work it out for herself. Still, Raan was right, the time to discuss it would be after they had landed.

"We're in range," Raan's voice cut into her thoughts.

"Try a distress call," ordered Erion.

"It's already on automatic," answered Starfire. "No response."

"Take her down anyway." she said.

"We haven't any choice in the matter, Major," began Raan, grimly. "We fly or we fall."

"Get me a soft landing site." called Starfire. Erion busied herself at the navi-com and punched in some co-ordinates. Starfire saw them come up on her heads up display and adjusted their trajectory.

Raan was right, it was a bumpy ride. The turbulence in the atmosphere didn't help matters either and Starfire and Raan had their hands full just keeping the craft on an even keel.

"Breaking thrusters," ordered Starfire.

"Malfunction," called Raan. "No brakes."

"Back up systems?" called Starfire, hopefully.

"Malfunction. No back up."

"Right then," grinned Starfire, wickedly. Time to see if all that simulator training paid off." Erion had guided them to a part of the planet that seemed mainly composed of sand and Starfire eased the big ship down, skimming the higher dunes. They dropped a little lower and the ship's belly hit the ground and bounced up again, throwing them about in their seats like rag dolls. They were slowing down, but another element had entered the game. Acrid smoke was rising from the controls, most of which showed red warning lights. Darker, thick smoke was creeping in through the hatchway and Starfire knew she must set the craft down before they went up like torch.

She altered their line of descent and they hit the sandy dunes harder. The ship jumped three times, skidded, jumped again and then slewed across the sand until it nose-dived into a hill. Starfire and Raan threw every switch non-op, Delta Ten had the extinguisher again and was making use of it when all the lights went out. There was much swearing and muttering until the dim emergency lighting came on and Erion gave a deep sigh.

"Well done you two."

"If you hadn't brought us to this desert, we'd be a pile of scrap," praised Starfire.

"Is everybody in one piece?" asked Raan. There were nods all round.

"Good," said Erion, "Status please Del."

"The ship has sustained sixty percent structural and electrical damage. The sand has put out the fire in the engine and the auto foam has extinguished the fires inside."

"Well at least we won't burn to death," said Raan. Del continued.

"The repair computers are damaged and off line, the air purifier is damaged and we are buried beneath the sand."

"What?" snapped Starfire.

"Augment," corrected Erion.

"The pilot section is totally buried beneath the sand, Major. The aft exit hatch is jammed, and the air purifier is working at twenty percent only."

"You mean we're trapped here?" asked Starfire.

"How long have we got?" asked Hal, getting to the point. As a logical thinking machine, Delta Ten should not have been able to answer that question, but since he had been in the company of humans, he had worked out for himself that they rarely said what they meant. He had taught himself to relay the last few sentences spoken and use his logic to predict what their next statement would be. He therefore deduced that the question pertained to the length of time the humans had before their air ran out and they ceased to function.

"If the present circumstances do not change," he said calmly, "the oxygen will run out in two point four nine hours.

CHAPTER 5

Everyone began speaking at once and Erion held up her hand and waited for silence to descend.

"Suggestions please, Del."

"Assuming that the General's theory is correct and there is sentient life on this planet, I suggest we contact the Serrellians and ask for their assistance."

"Is that all you can come up with?" asked Raan.

"It is the first thing we should do." stated the robot. "With the ship buried and the air purifier damaged, you must do as little as possible to conserve your oxygen supply. I do not need oxygen and I will endeavour to repair the purifier myself."

"While we just sit around conserving air," put in Hal.

"I know it is often infuriating," began Erion, "but Del is never wrong."

"Well he's wrong about contacting the Serrellians," growled Raan. "The com-link is out."

"That's just great!" snapped Starfire as she leaned over

Raan's shoulder to verify his statement. "He's right, No com-link."

"What do we do now tin brains?" asked Starfire. The robot did not know she was referring to him and it was Raan who answered.

"I say we try and get to the rear hold and see if we can dig out the Space suits. They have their own recycle units. It would give us more time."

"Is the way dear, Del?" asked Erion.

"The rear hold is directly behind the damaged engine." Delta Ten was pressing buttons as he spoke, communicating directly with the ship's computers. "The hold has been damaged by the fire, although the repair computers have put it out. If the suits are there, they may be too damaged to be of use."

"The top hatch then?" suggested Hal.

"According to the hull sensors, most of the forward section is buried under at least six feet of sand and the pressure on the top hatch would be too great for me to open it manually. Even if it was possible to open the hatch, the sand would pour into the ship and fill it before any air could enter. We can't open the belly cargo doors while the ship is lying flat and the rear hatch has suffered impact damage."

"There must be something we can do?" said Raan.

"Well this is coming off for a start," said Erion, flinging the wig into a corner. "If we're going to be dug up by a team of archaeologists in three hundred years time, I want to look my best."

"I say fly us out," stated Starfire. She had been quietly checking her status monitors and had wanted to be sure before she spoke.

"You're crazy," said Raan.

"Can you do it?" asked Hal.

"One way to find out," she answered, looking around her at all the amazed faces. "What other choices do we have?"

"None at present," answered the robot.

"Look, I've checked with the computers and it's probable the engines will fire. They won't give us lift, but maybe I can jiggle the ship about a bit and bounce us out. The forward breaking thrusters have malfunctioned so I can't use them so force us out backwards but....." Starfire hesitated,

"Well?" three voices asked in unison.

"This ship has two propulsion systems. Once in orbit, the neutron accelerator cuts in."

"We know that," put in Raan, then suddenly stopped as the same thought occurred to him.

"For lifting thrust," continued Starfire, "there are chemical rockets and they need…"

"Oxygen." snarled Hal.

"If we're going to do it, it'll have to be soon," warned Starfire. "I'll need to channel most of our remaining supply to the starboard engine to get it to fire."

"Do it then," ordered Erion. Command came naturally to her and she made the decision quite easily, but to her own amazement, she added, "Everyone agreed?"

"Sure," said Hal,

"I hope you know what you're doing," muttered Raan.

"It's too late for that now Captain," said Starfire, her final checks completed. "Get strapped in. Raan, give me a five down for primary ignition." Raan pressed a sequence of buttons on the co pilot's console and began to count.

"Five, four, three,," an ear piercing wail began, accompanied by a soft computerised female voice which said,

"Warning! You have activated primary igniters without sufficient fuel for lift off."

"Override the failsafe," snapped Starfire. She channelled their reserves of oxygen into the mixer tanks at the back of the ship, keeping an anxious eye on the fuel gauge. It stayed resolutely on zero.

"Here goes," she called, and pushed the throttles forward. The noise proof cladding must have been damaged in the pilot compartment, because the whine had now risen to a mighty roar and those who could, clapped their hands over their ears as the massive engine tried to force the ship forward with the weight of the sand upon it.

Starfire brought in the second, damaged engine and it spluttered faintly, cutting in and out to make the ship jolt and lurch. Raan yelled something to her, but she couldn't hear and he had to thump her arm to gain her attention. He pointed to one of the many flickering red displays in front of her. It was the fuel gauge empty warning. The computer added to the din with another of its warnings. They were low on oxygen.

"Transfer all remaining fuel to the lifting thrusters," she yelled to Raan, who nodded and complied. The damaged engine cut out and the ship started to buck and shudder violently. Starfire and Raan wrestled with the controls and the others could do nothing to help but sit in their seats and try to stop themselves being shaken about. It was becoming increasingly hot and the smell of burning circuitry permeated the crew compartment. Erion glanced across at Hal, who shrugged, calmly accepting his fate. She looked angrily away and caught sight of Starfire and Raan throwing switches non op and laughing with delight. The deafening din sank to a low whine and stopped.

"We made it," beamed Starfire. They felt the ship sink slightly and ominous sounds of groaning metal could be heard deep in the bowels of the hold. The wind blew a covering of fine sand from the direct viewing ports and bright sunlight filtered into the compartment. They sat for a few seconds in glorious silence, then Starfire said, "Well this thing's flying days are over unless there happens to be a class one star base on this planet."

"Let's get some air in here," began Erion. "Del, see if you can blow the top hatch. Raan, get down to the cargo bay and break out the ATV. Maybe we can find one for you." She motioned to Hal, "Go with him will you." To her amazement, the lean gun fighter stood up and followed the captain out. Erion smiled at Starfire. "Natural leadership," she explained. "Some of us have it, some of us don't."

"And some of us were going to check it out anyway," called Hal's voice from the corridor.

The sun was low in the sky as an eight wheeled truck pulled away from the freighter with Del at the controls. Starfire looked mournfully back at the wrecked ship and sighed. The rear bay door, situated underneath the two massive engines was too buckled to open, so they had spent the best part of four hours with a cutting torch to make a hole big enough to drive the vehicle out. It was a cumbersome, noisy thing, completely self contained and could travel at speed over land and water in very difficult conditions if it had to. The correct title for it was 'All Purpose Terrain Vehicle but was commonly shortened to 'ATV'. It was designed to cater fully for six people in reasonable comfort but with the extra rations and equipment they had stowed aboard, space was limited and it was decided that each of them should take a turn in the turret cannon to ease the crowding. Hal was up there at the moment and Starfire passed him up a cup of coffee.

"What can you see?" she asked, peering up into the transparent dome. The gunner had a direct, all round view of the outside world, while those inside the truck had to rely on holographic terrain scans and video pictures relayed to the consoles.

"Sand and rocks," came the grunted reply.

"Let's have a look," she begged and forced herself up into the tiny bubble to perch on Hal's knee. He did have a tendency to understate but in this instance, his description was spot on. "There's a tree!" she pointed out hopefully.

"It is dead," Delta Ten's voice drifted up.

"Are you always so negative?" she shouted down to him, climbing from her perch and choosing not to hear Hal's groan of relief. Although they knew a powerful shield generator was on the planet somewhere, they could pick up no signs of an energy field. For want of a better place, Delta Ten headed the ATV towards a distant line of hills. From the ancient maps they had, it seemed that the early settlers had chosen the mountainous region to set up their base and a thin, green line in the distance suggested some sort of vegetation at its base. It did seem a long shot, but nobody asked Del to quote the odds on finding intelligent life. Their scanners so far all read negative for that as well.

Although the ATV was equipped with light intensifying equipment, they decided to make camp before dark, wanting a chance to stretch their legs and breathe real air. Delta Ten stopped the truck at the foot of a small rocky outcrop and they all piled out to view the scenery first hand. The sun was sinking slowly behind the mountain range and cast a deep orange glow over the barren landscape. Erion suggested they eat outside, like the early pioneers must have done and Raan, who sensed that she was trying desperately to fit in with this group of weirdoes she had inherited, agreed wholeheartedly and began to carry tables and chairs outside. Once the sun had gone though, the portable lights and flickering fire created eerie shapes in the rocks and the wind whistled mournfully. They sat round the fire, eating their rations without relish and drinking coffee while Delta Ten set up the camp defences.

Hal stood up to light one of his thin black cigars, using a glowing twig from the fire. As he lifted the flame to the end of it, a warning chime sounded from within the ATV and he stiffened suddenly, the ember falling to the earth unheeded in a shower of sparks.

"What is it?" asked Raan, standing back from the table, his hand reaching for the laser carbine leaning by his chair. Hal waved him into silence, his narrowed eyes raking the rocks around them.

"The computers have picked up life signs," explained Erion, quietly. Delta Ten walked into the circle of light.

"A group of humans is approaching the camp," he said.

"Hostile?" asked Erion.

"They are hidden from view," he answered, "Although I can hear them moving towards us through the rocks."

"Take up defensive positions," snapped Erion, picking up her own carbine, "We'll..."

A hideous yell cut short her sentence and a muscular, filthy man, dressed in rags and furs hurtled towards them, unfortunately for him, straight into Hal's line of fire. He fell in two pieces at Starfire's feet but she was too busy to notice as several others joined him, jumping down from the rocks above. Erion had landed in a tangled heap with her assailant. Lifting a shapely leg, she put her foot in his stomach and pushed hard. He flew over her head and rolled quickly to his feet, wielding a long bladed flint knife with expertise. He launched himself at her with a roar that was supposed to freeze her into immobility. It didn't work and Erion, taking careful aim, shot him through the chest. His dead body shot backwards and cannoned into Starfire, who was taking aim at her opponent. She cursed as her hand gun spun from her grasp and leapt backwards as he slashed at her with a knife. She sucked in her belly and bent forwards, swearing afterwards that she felt the wind of the blade as it just missed her stomach. The savage changed tactics and held his knife with the blade held downwards, aiming for a chop against her neck. Quick as a flash, her left hand shot out and the back of her wrist deflected his bony arm aside. She sent her right hand flying up to the nape of her neck, where a little laser dagger nestled in a sheath under her hair. Her hand reappeared, whipped across the savage's throat and a thin blue beam sliced his neck through to the bone. He fell at her feet with a gurgle, rolled slowly over and jerked once as a blast from Raan's carbine caught him.

"You all right?" he called, tossing her the carbine and bringing out his hand gun with practiced ease. She nodded and turned the weapon in an arc to look for a fresh target, but it was strangely quiet.

"They've gone," stated Hal flatly from his pile of bodies, his narrowed eyes taking in every detail. They stood and looked around, stunned at the carnage until Hal grabbed a savage by the ankles and started to haul him out of camp. As he passed Raan he gritted, "Could use some help, flyboy."

"Sure," he answered, grabbing the body under it's arms. They staggered off into the darkness, closely followed by Delta Ten, who had one slung over his shoulder. Erion and Starfire looked at each other, took a deep breath and followed suit, carrying another stinking body out of camp. Over an hour later, they sat exhausted and drank more coffee, while Delta Ten reset the camp perimeter defences. Hal stood up, threw his dregs into the sand, muttered,

"I'm turning in," and walked to the truck without a backward glance.

"How do you think he does that?" asked Starfire.

"A natural killer," answered Erion. "I suppose it's all in a day's work for him. I wonder if there's anything that would put him off his sleep."

"People stealing his cigars perhaps," whispered Starfire, holding up a thin black variety and twirling it twixt finger and thumb. It must have fallen out of his pocket in the fight. I'd love to light it up, but I daren't in case he catches me and shoots my head off."

"Go ahead," said Hal's voice from inside the truck. Starfire caught Raan's pleading eye and smiled.

"We'll share it," she said, accepting a light from him. Another cigar flew from the open door of the truck and landed on the table in front of Raan. He lit it with a grin and sucked in the aromatic smoke with a satisfied sigh.

"Thanks pal," he said, but Hal was already asleep.

CHAPTER 6

It was late when Delta Ten woke them the next morning, and after a quick breakfast of cereal bars and coffee, they broke camp and set off towards the hills again. The air conditioning in the truck ensured their comfort although it was extremely hot and dry outside. A quick check by Delta Ten informed him that they would have to find water within two days so Erion plotted them a new course, still towards the line of hills, but at a less direct angle, where the logic computers and scanners suggested there might be some. The terrain began to change and they found the ground becoming less sandy and more rocky. The main vegetation seemed to consist of low, twisted trees with tiny, dark green leaves, something between a cordwood tree and a prickly cactus.

Eventually Delta Ten stopped the ATV at the base of the foothills and Starfire, who was at the scanner console, announced to all that they had scored a hit.

"There's water in them there hills; 2 kliks away, 240 west-six."

"Good," muttered Erion, "I hope there's enough for a bath." Delta Ten took a hover trolley and strode purposely off to find water while Raan cut some more wood to make a fire. Once this was done, Starfire, Erion and Raan sat around the computer output screen, sifting through the information that Delta Ten had set up for them while they were all asleep. Using data and passwords given to him by General Dubois, the android had managed to amass quite a store of classified facts about the colonisation mission to Serrell.

"There were some good techs among them." exclaimed Raan. "Look there, a physicist and a biochemist.

"Engineers too," put in Starfire. "They must have made quite a team." She caught Hal's eye and grinned. "I wonder if they met any Dragons." The gunman pulled a wry face and carried on cleaning his guns.

"Dragons?" asked Erion.

"It's an old fairy tale," explained Starfire. "A bedtime story. Dragons live here in the caves and fly to Terrell in search of naughty children. If they find any, they carry them off in a fiery chariot and eat them."

"So scaring tiny children out of their wits just before they go to sleep is an acceptable form of child rearing on Terrell is it then?" asked Erion.

"It's only a story!" muttered Starfire, resenting any criticism of her home planet, unless it was done by her, of course.

"If you don't mind," sniffed Erion, "Let's get back to the matter in hand shall we?" She pressed another button on the computer console and the screen filled with information. They all stared intently at it, then looked at each other.

"Nothing makes sense," said Raan.

"As far as the records go, standard contact was maintained

until three weeks before the explosion," said Starfire. "There's nothing here to show any conflict. It must have been an accident."

"I suppose we'll never know," answered Erion.

"Very convenient for the Electorate on Terrell at the time though," mused Raan. "These savages can't be the ones behind the attacks on Terrell; they're too primitive. The Serrellians fighting this war are supposed to be high-tech. They have this planet ray shielded."

"There are no native Serrellians," said Erion. "So these savages must be settlers' descendants. Where are the high-tech people?"

"What if some of the original scientists saved themselves somehow," suggested Starfire. "Maybe they went underground and started a Terrellian type base."

"Where would they get the equipment to do that?" asked Raan."

"And why not just make contact?" asked Erion. "Why declare war all of a sudden?" A loud crack rent the air and they all jumped and turned to see Hal snap the barrel of his pistol back onto its charger grip. He gave a cold grin and answered Erion's question.

"Revenge!"

"I might know you'd come up with an answer," muttered Erion.

"The shield was down," pointed out Starfire, "So someone let us through and I don't think it could have been those natives." At that moment, Delta Ten arrived with large water barrels to replenish their stock. All conversation ceased while they helped connect the pipes which would pump the liquid up to the storage tanks on the roof of the ATV. It was getting dark and a light breeze brought welcome respite from the dry heat of the day. The crew sat outside in their porta-chairs and continued the debate.

"I still don't understand why they haven't made contact with us," said Erion. "They must know we're here."

"Maybe the shield was down for someone else?" suggested Raan.

"No," discounted Erion. "They must have been tracking us."

"Maybe they're waiting for us to make the first move," suggested Starfire.

"We'll just have to keep looking," said Erion. She lifted her head to gaze out over the barren landscape. "It's too late to move on but it's too early to turn in." Hal stood up and brushed past her.

"I'll take a scout around." He walked out of camp before anyone could say anything.

"It was his turn to wash the dishes," grumbled Starfire. She caught the stares of the other two and went to finish the task herself. "They never show you this in the recruit holos."

"Stop complaining," called Erion, "All you have to do is put them in the cleaner."

"Del should be doing this, not me," she answered. "I'm supposed to be the Pilot Five here."

"And also a Lieutenant," pointed out Raan. He emerged from the truck holding a pack of playing cards which he placed on the table and shuffled with fancy dexterity.

"I thought we weren't going to do the rank pulling thing," muttered Starfire. Task completed, she joined the others but declined a game of cards. She watched Raan and Erion play a couple of hands of Pan but soon became bored. The sun set, and although Serrell had no moons, the huge crescent of its sister planet, Terrell, was just beginning to show itself on the horizon and the sky was littered with many stars. It looked very dark away from the glare of their portable lights and Hal had still not returned when Raan looked at his wrist comlink.

"It's been well over an hour. I'm going out to look for him."

"Hal can take care of himself," said Erion.

"I know," agreed Raan, but the son of a bitch is too good of a shot for us to loose."

"I'll go," put in Starfire, walking to the truck and grabbing a torch. "It won't take me long to pick up his trail; I'll just follow the cigar butts." She picked up a carbine and slung it over her shoulder. Raan made to object but Erion said.

"Let her go, she knows what she's doing." She lifted her hand to Starfire in silent salute and watched her walk out of camp. Starfire answered her with a nod and headed out towards the base of the rocks. She met Delta Ten on his way in and told him where she was going.

"Let me come with you?" suggested the handsome android.

"No thanks, Del. We can't all start wandering round in the dark. Your job is to look after the camp. If we loose our transport and equipment out here we might as well be dead. I'll be okay, I have my carbine." Starfire walked purposely forward, looking much braver than she felt. Hal's footprints could no longer be seen as she climbed up into the rocks. She worked her way steadily upwards for half an hour then tried to raise him on her wrist com-link. "Hal?" she whispered, "Come in will you." There was no answer and no indication on the hand held movement scanner she had brought with her. Hal was either motionless or out of range. She needed both hands to climb now, so she put the scanner in her tote and slung the carbine across her back, out of easy reach. She regretted this action a few minutes later, when a strong hand forced itself over her mouth and stifled her outcry.

"Easy, easy, it's me," whispered Hal into her ear.

"What the hell do you think you're doing?" she hissed at him, "I nearly died of fright!"

"Will you shut up!" he mouthed back at her. He grabbed her wrist and dragged her to a narrow ledge. He placed a long finger over her lips and mimed her forward. They crept towards the edge and looked down into a torch lit valley. Forty feet below them was a small encampment. They could dimly hear chattering coming from natives who sat around a large fire, burning brightly in the centre of a group of crude mud huts. Hal and Starfire pulled back from the rim.

"They look like the same ones who attacked us." said Starfire quietly.

"They can't be," began Hal, "unless they have a means of transport."

"They don't look like the people we've been sent to find at all," mused Starfire.

"There's something not right here," Hal was thinking aloud. "Let's get back to the truck and talk this out. Come on and be quiet!" It was much harder going down and almost two hours passed before they walked towards their camp site.

"Where are the lights?" whispered Starfire, unslinging her carbine. Everywhere was dark and silent. They separated, going into the camp from opposing directions, guns drawn and ready. They met in the approximate centre of their camp and stared about in amazed silence. The camp was empty.

"Are you sure this is the right place?" asked Starfire, swinging her torch in a wide arc. It earned her a dirty look and Hal took the torch from her and pointed it at a portable scanner

Delta Ten had placed in the rocks above them.

"They must have left in a hell of a hurry," he mused. "They didn't pick up the perimeter defence scanners."

"They wouldn't have left us behind if they had any choice in the matter," stated Starfire defiantly.

"They left us this, though." Hal showed her a small survival pack "Tracks go off that way," he said, shining the beam of his torch along the heavy tyre marks of several vehicles.

"Do we follow them?" asked Starfire.

"Not tonight. We'll get some sleep, then head for that village in the morning, see if we can steal some food and water before we start." Cold wind stirred the sand and he grabbed her elbow and steered her towards the relative shelter of the rocks. "Come on Lieutenant, let's see how your survival training pays off in the real world."

CHAPTER 7

Raan watched Starfire leave, then shuffled the pack again.
"Do you play Pan?" he asked.
"Of course," answered Erion. "What shall we play for?"
"Clothes?" asked Raan hopefully.
"How about a credit a hand?" suggested Erion with a grin. "I'll keep score." She shivered slightly. "Let's get into the truck. It's warmer there and Del can keep watch." It took Raan just a few hands to realise that, should they have been playing for clothes, he would have been the one naked and shivering, not Erion.
"How much do I owe you now?" he asked.
"Everything you have, if I have counted this right," she smiled.
"How long have the others been gone?" asked Raan, trying to change the subject.
"Over two hours," she said worriedly. "Too long." She summoned Delta Ten and he appeared almost immediately. He bowed and began to speak, but a computer warning cut him off.

"Intruder alarm," snapped Raan.

"Is it Starfire?" asked Erion.

"No, it is a vehicle of some kind," answered Delta Ten.

"I'm on it," called Raan from the laser turret. The warning bleeps sounded again.

"Another one," called Erion from her post. "We're in a cross fire angle. Del, keep watch while I set the aft lasers. Raan, you keep your guns trained forward."

"Sure," he called from the gun turret.

"The intruder requests communication." informed Delta Ten.

"Patch me in then." began Erion. "Let's see who they are and what they want. These might very well be the people we're looking for." She pressed a button in front of her, composed herself and began to speak as Erion Dune, the Dancer. "Hello, yes, what do you want?"

"We wish to extend greetings to you and your party," said a male voice. It sounded warm, genuine and educated. Erion caught Delta Ten's eye. It certainly looked like they were on the right track. The voice continued. "We wish to extend to you our hospitality and suggest you join us in the safety of our base."

"We're fine, we don't need any help," called Erion, not wishing to seem too eager. They were after all supposed to be on the run, and not given to trusting strangers.

"Listen miss," the voice was beginning to sound strained. "May I come into camp and speak to you and your party directly. I assure you that you are in great danger and the longer you remain here the worse it will get." Erion shut off the link for a few seconds, sighed heavily, jammed the long wig on her head then switched it on again, as if she had been in conference with her friends.

"Okay then, but just you alone and no weapons!"

"Very well," he answered, and Delta Ten informed her that one lone man was walking into their camp. Raan put the spotlights on him for a better view.

"Scan for weapons," instructed Erion.

"Scan negative," answered Delta Ten.

"He's reached us." began Raan, "Shall I open the hatch?"

"Yes, Raan, but keep a close watch on the rest of them. I doubt whether they'll try anything with their friend in here, but you never know. I get the feeling these guys don't play fair."

"You got it," answered Raan. The hatch opened and a young man stepped elegantly into the truck, apparently unconcerned at Erion's laser rifle aimed at his middle.

"My name is Keen, secretary to Councillor Greeb." he began, "I am here to escort your party to safety."

"Safety from what?" asked Raan from his position in the turret.

"As you know, there are wandering bands of nomads in this area. All of them are hostile." The young man seemed very sure of himself, and Erion had the distinct feeling that they had been watched from the very moment they had landed on the planet. She threw Raan a warning glance and said.

"We haven't seen anything of them."

"My dear," began Keen, 'We have been watching your progress closely." You have already staved off one attack. You have been very lucky. Might I also remind you that had we not switched off our screens, you would have burned up in our shields."

"You mean you knew we were in trouble and didn't t help us?" asked Erion.

"You must understand, we had to be sure you were not sent

from Terrell to spy on us. We let you through our screens and watched you crash on our planet. I assure you we would not have let you die. I must say your pilot is very experienced. Your work?"

"No," said Erion, "That was Starfire. She is out there with Hal. They have been gone too long. Can you find them for us?" Erion looked so pathetic that Raan had to look away in case he caught her eye.

"We will return to our base and look for them with our scanners," said Keen.

"No way!" snapped Raan. "They have no all weather gear. We can't just leave them out here."

"I appreciate your concern for your friends, Captain, but I assure you we can best help your friends from our base. It is far too dangerous to look for them now."

"We are receiving a signal from the first vehicle," broke in Delta Ten from his post. "They request communications."

"They will be concerned for my safety," said Keen. May I speak with them?"

"Go ahead," said Erion, shrugging her shoulders.

"This is Keen," began the young man, "I am alright. What have you to report?"

"Natives heading this way in large numbers, Sir."

"Can we out gun them?" asked Keen, worriedly.

"No sir," answered the voice.

"What do you mean, you can't outgun them?" asked Raan. "They haven't any guns."

"As I said, you have been lucky," said Keen hurriedly. "These creatures know no fear. In the past they have attacked and kept coming until our guns have lost power. They have lost hundreds of their warriors, but they will keep coming until they breach our defences. You must believe me and come with us, or I am afraid I must leave you here and take my own men to safety."

"But Starfire and Hal...." began Raan.

"Your friends are more than likely dead already." Keen was beginning to look frightened and he wasn't that good an actor. "Even if you stay here you will not be able to save them. Your only chance is to come with us."

"I am detecting life forms heading this way," said Delta Ten quietly. "They are in extreme range and will be within attacking distance in four point two minutes." Erion and Raan looked at each other. Raan sighed and looked down, shaking his head.

"You must also be aware that you are caught in a crossfire configuration. You don't really have much choice in the matter."

"We have you," pointed out Raan. Keen gestured towards the comlink and Erion stood aside for him.

"Lieutenant Randal, what are your orders?"

"To open fire on the ATV in two minutes time whether you are aboard or not, sir."

"All right Mr Keen, you win." said Erion grimly. We will come with you. Would you like to stay with us or return to your own car."

"I'd like to get back to my men," began Keen, bowing slightly. He spoke into the com link, "I'm coming out, Lieutenant. We're heading back to base. Keep tracking those savages."

"Yes, Sir," There was obvious relief in the other's voice.

"Please follow the first car." instructed Keen. He stopped at the door and raised his second in command again. "Lieutenant, please contact the scanner room at Control and have them scan for…"

"A Terrellian man and woman," supplied Raan.

"What weapons are they carrying?" asked Keen.

"Laser carbine and laser bolt hand gun," called Raan. This information was relayed to the faceless Lieutenant and Keen left the ATV, running towards the forward vehicle. It had begun to turn around as soon as Keen had contacted it and while it was in the process of doing so, Erion flung a survival pack out of the ATV into the blackness beyond the lights. Delta Ten started their truck moving and the second troop carrier waited until they had gone by before pulling out behind them. They were bracketed and could do nothing but follow the truck in front. Raan climbed down from the turret to sit with Erion and gaze into the hologram screens to chart their progress. Direct viewing was impossible in the total darkness, but the scanners could work in those conditions and relayed holograms to the inside of the truck that gave a stylised view of the world around them. They had been travelling for nearly three hours across the rough terrain when Delta Ten looked up from his console.

"Erion, we seem to be heading straight for the side of a mountain."

"Do not be alarmed," Keen's voice called over the comlink. The first car reached the cliff and disappeared. They followed and saw the structure of the rocks dissipate as they approached. Suddenly they were through and driving down a dimly lit tunnel large enough for two of their trucks to pass with no difficulty.

"Very neat," mused Raan, impressed despite himself. "I've never seen a shield holo that big. No wonder there's no trace of this place with scanners. It must take some power." They travelled steadily for a couple of minutes, heading on a slightly downward path all the way. The car in front started to slow down and Delta Ten was instructed to pull into a vacant space in the vehicle park. It was light and clean and very modern looking everywhere and reminded Erion of Central City on her home planet. She was about to remark upon this point when Keen spoke on the comlink.

"I am sure you would like to rest after your long journey. I ask you to comply with our request that all weapons be left aboard your ATV. You may lock your vehicle and I assure you nothing will be touched." Clearly this did not go down well with Raan whose hand flew to the gun at his side. He set his jaw and shook his head.

"No one takes my gun."

"Captain, ask your driver to scan the immediate area. Due to the nature of our work here, you will find no one carrying weapons."

"He is correct." supplied Delta Ten.

"I still don't like it," snarled Raan. Erion caught his eye and tried to convey something to him without Keen picking up on it.

"Raan, honey, I'm tired and I'm sick of running. Why can't you just take off the dammed gun and let's go meet the man who saved our lives." It was Erion the Dancer talking and Raan received the message loud and clear. They had come too far now to cause a scene. She stepped close to him and purred, "Please Raan, For me?" Then she hissed in his ear so that Keen could not catch it, "We're supposed to be among friends. Now act like it!"

"Sure honey." smiled Raan, unbuckling the heavy gun belt and letting it slide downwards. He caught it with his other hand and placed it gently on a vacant seat. "Let's get this show on the road." They alighted from the truck and Delta Ten locked it before joining the others on a small, rubber wheeled ground trolley. It set silently off along many twists and turns, obviously designed to confuse them and make returning to the truck difficult. However Delta Ten had already planned a route map for their return. He calculated that although they had been travelling for over twenty minutes, they were less than a thousand metres from their original position. The vehicle stopped outside a plain, white door and Keen alighted from the little cart, opened the door with a card key and motioned them inside. The room was furnished in the same bland style as a hotel suite and Keen pointed out the twin beds, couch and bathroom.

"Make yourselves comfortable. Our leader has asked to see you after you have rested and eaten. I will return in seven hours."

"Well, the fact that we haven't been blasted into space yet gives me some comfort." Raan threw himself onto a settee and helped himself to a ration bar from a bowl on a side table.

"Going for a look around is out," stated Erion from the door. "We're locked in." They both looked at Delta Ten, who nodded quickly. The room was bugged.

"Might as well get some shut eye, then," began Raan, patting the settee on the vacant cushion next to him. "Come on, honey and give old Raan a hug."

"Sure, sugar," gritted Erion, pasting a smile on her features as she snuggled up to him.

"Just you wait, Captain," she hissed into his ear as she nuzzled his neck. Raan gave her a dazzling smile and held her close.

"Just like old times, babe."

Keen was true to his word and entered their rooms without knocking exactly seven hours later.

"I see you are refreshed," he eyed Erion, who was still dressed as a dancer, with a smirk.

"Yeah, we're good to go," Raan stepped protectively in front of her as if she was his possession. Smiling as if he knew something they did not, Keen motioned them outside where another little trolley car was waiting. They climbed in and it set off soundlessly, not needing a driver. The car stopped a few minutes later, Keen stepped out of it and held his hand ready for Erion to take. They had pulled into a private parking bay outside tall double doors. They slid open at Keen's touch to reveal an anti room where a hard faced Aurian woman sat behind a reception desk. She nodded to Keen, pressed a button on her console and said,

"Your guests are here, Sir."

"Send them in, Vander," She pressed another button and a door opened to their right.

"Please go in." she said and Keen motioned them forward. They entered the room to see a large Aurian man sitting behind a desk. He rose to greet them and stepped from behind it, his large hands reaching out to take Erion's.

"No," said Raan, softly. Erion looked swiftly sideways at him, worried by his expression.

"Oh, don't stand on ceremony, Captain Raan," said the fat man. "Introduce me to the lady."

"I'd sooner introduce her to a wanga."

"Do you know this man, Raan, honey?" asked Erion, still in the guise of the dancer. Raan gave a deep sigh and spoke reluctantly.

"Erion, Del, meet Dolton Blass."

CHAPTER 8

Starfire shivered and huddled nearer to the lean gun fighter, trying to keep warm. Dark grey cloud covered most of the sky, Terrell only visible now as a slightly lighter glow above the horizon. Without its brilliance in the night sky, the darkness was almost absolute and she didn't like the idea of temporary blindness. They had switched off the torches, not knowing if they might need the valuable energy in its batteries to recharge their guns.

"Can't you keep still?" grunted Hal, as Starfire tried to make herself more comfortable. Rather than pitch the lightweight tent Erion had thrown from the ATV, they wrapped it around themselves and sat with their backs against the rocks in a small depression out of the wind. It was rocky, cold and comfortless in the darkness but Hal, as usual, had managed to fall asleep.

"It's alright for you," she grumbled, "but I'm not made of steel." His hand closed over her wrist with such force that she almost cried out but his words silenced any outburst.

"There's something out there. Get up slow and easy and be ready with the torch when I say." They shrugged out of the tent as quietly as they could and Starfire sensed rather than saw him standing by her side in the darkness. She heard the faint sound of him drawing his gun and reached for the button to switch on the torch.

"Now," he hissed and she switched it on, gasping at the sight that met their eyes. Over twenty natives surrounded them, standing like statues with glittering eyes and stone age weapons gripped in sinewy hands. They must have been steadily creeping up on them for hours, one of them making a slight sound which had alerted Hal. No fool, the latter dropped his gun and raised his hands above his head, instructing Starfire to do the same. They were hopelessly outnumbered but with any luck, a chance to escape would present itself sooner or later.

The natives lit brush torches and walked closer to inspect their captives and relieve them of their possessions. A huge bear like man with only one ear reached out for Starfire and pulled her forward with a leering grin. She bunched her fist and slammed it into his middle with all her might. It was like hitting a wooden plank and she gasped in pain, rubbing her knuckles and letting out a strangled curse. This action seemed to delight the man and he grabbed her by her hair and shoved her into the centre of a group of savages. Hal was pushed roughly after her and landed in a crumpled heap at her feet. She lent him a hand to rise and they both submitted to having their wrists tied behind their backs with coarse rope. The little they could see of their captors proved that they were probably from the same species that had attacked their camp the night before. They certainly smelled the same as Starfire could testify. The large brutish one eared man was taller than all the others and seemed to be their leader. He mimed them forward with a grunt and pushed Hal roughly in the back with the blunt end of his spear bringing him to the ground with a thud. The others thought this was most amusing and loud guffaws greeted Hal's attempts to rise as the one eared thug prodded him back to ground with the wooden staff.

Starfire couldn't quite see what was happening, but somehow, Hal made it to his feet and planted a hard kick on his assailant's shin. From the awed gasps of the onlookers, it was clear that the brute demanded unthinking obedience from his followers and the retaliation took him by completely by surprise. With a huge bellow, he swung a hairy fist which lifted Hal from his feet and sent him crashing back into the dust. Hal picked himself up and made a mental note to place the brute on the top of his payback list.

They walked for over an hour, stumbling over the rocks and sand, too tired to talk and concentrating on keeping their balance. The party turned into a high narrow crevice in the rocks which widened out into a canyon and eventually emerged at the base of the cliff Hal and Starfire had been leaning over the night before. There was a great commotion at their appearance and they were led to the large central hut where all the villagers amassed to peruse them. Vision was improving with the rising sun and Hal could see they were in a lot of trouble. Still, he had been in worse spots and survived. A quick glance across at Starfire showed she was holding up well and not showing anything of the fear she must be feeling. If anything, she looked angry and Hal caught her eye and grinned in an effort to boost her confidence. To Starfire, it looked like he was cracking up under the strain and her spirits plummeted.

A sudden hush descended upon the crowd as a large bearded

man and a short, muscular woman stepped out of the hut. Both had long light brown, dirty hair that tumbled over their shoulders and wore filthy, rancid furs. The man's face was disfigured and warped, one eye much lower than the other. He wore Hal's gun belt around his waist and the woman was carrying Starfire's carbine like a bunch of flowers in front of her. It didn't take a genius to figure out that this was the Head Man and his First Lady. He swaggered forward, peering closely at Starfire, who reeled back from the smell of him. He roared with laughter and grabbed her upper arm, intending to haul her off in the direction of his hut. Hal received the same attention from the man's good lady, and after some violent bickering, where Starfire was pulled this way and that between them, like a sale bargain, Head Man gave his consent and presented Hal to the woman. She cackled loudly and ran her claw like hands over his black shirt, feeling the soft material between her fingers. He in turn studied her closely, seeing that she was built like a wrestler, but he figured he could out match her if he could get to Starfire's light blade and free his hands before his fingers turned blue and dropped off.

The sound of fighting from came from inside the hut and Hal heard Starfire yell an obscenity followed by the sound of smashing pottery. The watchers were greatly amused by this and there was much nudging and pointing. Hal forced himself to remain calm as Starfire screamed and then there was silence. The smelly woman favoured Hal with a toothless grin and pointed to the hut, making a universal obscene gesture. He smiled back, looking very handsome and very innocent. Still smiling he said,

"If you've hurt her in any way, I'll kill you both, you see if I don't." The woman nodded her assent and, babbling away in a foreign tongue, pulled him to the now silent hut. 'What a way to go' he thought to himself as he bent low and shouldered his way inside, admitting to himself that there just might be a fate worse than death.

Hal squinted his eyes to adjust to the gloom inside. It was dank and squalid with no windows, but light filtered down in a dusty beam from a hole in the roof that served as a chimney for the dead fire in the centre of the hut. There was a pile of rancid smelling furs to one side, on which the man lay, moaning softly, but there was no sign of Starfire. The same thought occurred to the woman and she opened her mouth to bellow something but Hal lowered his head and butted her in the stomach. Her foul breath gushed forth and she doubled over with a croak. Starfire slammed shut the wooden planked door and sprang forward from where she had been behind it. Hal leaned on the door to prevent the woman's escape while Starfire grabbed a large pot and brought it down upon the woman's head. It broke with a loud crash and she fell to the floor unconscious.

"Let's get loose before they come to." gasped Starfire. She had managed to bring her hands to the front of her body but they were still tied together. There was an agonising minute while Hal tried to reach the laser dagger at the back of her neck with his teeth. He finally managed it and Starfire took it in her hands, lighting the blade to slice the ropes that bound Hal. Ignoring the pain caused by restoring his circulation, he returned the favour and they searched the hut for something to tie up the native couple. The man looked decidedly green and Starfire admitted that she had let him feel her knee bone in a place where it would do the most harm. His one eared Lieutenant had been over zealous in his use of the rope and it had cut deep into his Hal's wrists, rubbing away the skin to leave deep, raw wounds. He brushed Starfire's concern aside and motioned to the little dagger.

"How much power has that thing left? he asked.

"It had a full charge," she answered. "It won't have used much cutting through those ropes."

"Will it cut through the back of this hut," asked Hal, studying the rough clay walls."

"It should do," said Starfire as she studied the mud and straw walls.

"We'll wait until dark, then cut our way out and try to slip away."

"It's going to be a long wait," began Starfire. "What if someone comes to the hut?"

"We'll have to hope they don't," answered Hal. He felt decidedly better once his gun belt was strapped around his waist and he settled the big blaster inside its holster before easing himself down to sit with his back to the wall. "Try and get some sleep."

"Is there anywhere you can't sleep?" asked Starfire as the gunfighter crossed his arms and closed his eyes with a contented sigh.

"Yeah," he muttered, "Next to you."

"Very funny," glared Starfire, sitting down to keep a watch on the man and woman who lay bound and gagged on their pile of skins. She jumped as someone tried the door. Hal had placed a log across it but someone still tried to push it open. The door was rattled three or four times, then Hal picked up a rough clay bowl and threw it at the door, roaring something intelligible. The pottery smashed on impact and whoever it was gave up and went away. Starfire and Hal caught each other's eye and breathed a sigh of relief. They would not have been so self assured if they had noticed of the expressions on the faces of their captives, for they were gloating and triumphant. Hal settled back down to his snooze and Starfire leaned back against a strut, still keeping watch on the natives. Time passed and the stench in the hut seemed to grow with the rising heat of the day.

"I don't think I can stick it out in here all day," she muttered, wrinkling her nose in distaste. Her wish was granted for as Hal opened his mouth to answer her, the door burst open and natives spilled into the hut. Hal's gun appeared in his fist and he shot two of the men before Starfire could collect her thoughts. She reached for her carbine but it was a futile gesture as half naked savages poured into the hut from the doorway and dropped through the hole in the roof to engulf them. Hal saw Starfire disappear beneath a mound of bodies but he had troubles of his own. Four men lay dead at his feet, but sheer weight of numbers pushed him backwards. He stumbled and fell, shooting another savage before his gun was knocked from his hand. A heavy blow to the back of his head stunned him and he dropped forward onto his hands and knees to meet the up swinging foot of the one eared brute who had tripped him with his spear on their walk to the camp.

Hal shot backwards to measure his length across the floor. His vision blurred, but he could make out the grinning giant looming above him, raising his foot to smash it into Hal's face. Hal rolled to one side and grabbed his fallen weapon and bringing it into line while still on his back. He fired quickly, rubbing out the man from his payback list. Set for close work, the weapon sent a laser charge ripping into the savage It caught him under the chin and his faceless corpse shot upwards, hit the roof of the hut and rebounded on top of a group of terrified natives who were backing away. Just as Hal prepared to take advantage of this new turn of events, his attention switched to his right wrist, which was pinned to the ground by the Head Man's foot. Waves of pain shot up Hal's arm and his fingers opened to drop his gun. He saw the Head Man pick up the discarded weapon and he steeled himself for the shot but it didn't come. Teetering on the brink of consciousness, he felt himself lifted and carried out into the bright sunshine. His blurred vision tracked something that should not have been there and he fainted with a puzzled expression on his face.

Hal woke with a blinding headache and tried to move but his hands were tied behind his back again. The pain in his wrists made the headache seem less and he squinted his eyes to look across at Starfire who was similarly tied. They had been placed outside the hut and the sun was low in the sky, making it well past noon. Seeing he was awake, Starfire tried to crawl over to him. One of their guards jabbed her with the sharp end of his spear, making her gasp in pain. She crawled quickly to Hal, making her watchers laugh with glee.

"Take it easy," croaked Hal as Starfire fought to gain control of her shattered nerves.

"You were out so long, I thought they'd killed you," she said.

"Well they didn't," muttered Hal, not liking the thought of anyone caring about him. In fact, Hal had been wondering why they were still alive, although he didn't confide his thoughts to Starfire. They both looked up as the Head Man approached. Starfire must have given him a good whack because he could still hardly walk. He leered above them, pointing and babbling venomously in his own tongue. He motioned to his followers who rushed forward to haul them to their feet. They were herded roughly away from the huts towards a flat stone that jutted up from the ground and stood taller than a man. They were placed in front of it and secured back to back, while villagers walked forward and reverently placed their weapons on a bed of leaves at their feet. The crowd began to chant and parted for the Head Man and his Lady to walk to the front.

"We're going to be some sort of sacrifice!" gasped Starfire.

"Bend your knees," snapped Hal, refusing to give up, "See if you can reach my gun."

"I can't get to it," answered Starfire, as a blinding light engulfed them. "It's a force field." she snapped, "What the…" A grey green mist rose lazily from the ground and they felt their senses reeling.

"Gas," said Hal softly as he tried to fight it. They sagged gently at the knees and they were both unconscious before they slid to the ground and disappeared.

CHAPTER 9

"Dolton Blass?" blurted out Erion, "I thought you were dead!"

"Apparently, you have been misinformed, my dear," smiled Blass, walking from behind his desk to ooze in her direction. He touched palms with Erion, gripping her hand with his podgy fingers until she managed to slide herself free from his sweaty grasp.

"I saw your body being brought out of the hotel," said Raan.

'What you saw, Captain, was a well made double acting the part for me. I thought he was quite convincing. He was well paid for it too. Pity he didn't live long enough to spend his money."

"It sure fooled Hal," muttered Raan. The mention of the Terrellian gunfighter drove all traces of humour from Blass's face.

"We are still searching for Hal. When we find him, I will have the greatest pleasure in killing him myself." He saw the look on Erion's face and continued, "There's no need to worry about him my dear, I assure you he isn't dead yet."

"Even though your scanners can't pick them up?" she asked.

"Hal is a hard man to kill. Many have tried and failed," he snarled "until now." With a visible effort, Blass brought a smile to his face. "Enough about that Terrellian scum. Let us retire to the dining room. I am sure you must be hungry after your adventures." He started to leave, then turned when he saw the others weren't following him. The smile melted away, "I am trying to be patient."

"Look," snarled Raan, "Just stop messing us about and tell us what you're going to do."

"Kill you of course," smiled Dolton Blass. "But to tell you the truth, I don't get much in the way of intelligent company here. We might as well be as pleasant as possible about it." He walked over to Erion and held out his arm. She made no move to take it and his voice hardened. "You might as well amuse me; you will stay alive that little bit longer." Raan made a move to cut in, but caught Erion's warning head shake and stayed back. "Very wise, Captain Raan. "In fact I think I'll keep little Erion all to myself." Blass pressed a button on his console. "Vander, I will be dining with Miss Dune in my suite. Will you see to it that Mr Del and Captain Raan are shown to their quarters?" He snapped shut the link as the hard faced woman entered carrying a small hand gun. She motioned them to one side with the weapon and they stood back to allow Erion and Dolton Blass to walk past them to another doorway.

"Erion?" began Delta Ten, his programming at odds with his orders.

"It's alright, Del; stay with Raan. She suddenly felt as though she would never see them again and twisted her head around. "See you on the other side." She smiled as Raan threw her a saucy wink and she walked out of the room on Dolton Blass's arm without a backward glance. The woman called Vander watched all this without emotion. She pointed to the outer office and they walked in front of her. Two men in black and silver tunics were waiting there and took over from Vander, showing the two out of the office and back into the hover car, They were driven to another room and motioned inside. It contained two small cots with a table between them, upon which were two cold meals in plastic trays. A quick check proved the door to be locked and Delta Ten scanned for listening devices and hidden cameras while Raan ate the food.

"The surveillance devices have been deactivated," stated the android.

"Good," answered Raan. "We won't have much time before they come here to fix them again. We have to get out of here and blow this place."

"There is a guard outside," pointed out Del.

"Just get the door open," hissed Raan. "I'll deal with the guard." Walking to the door, Delta Ten placed his fingers over the locking mechanism and emitted a high pitched sonic beam that triggered the opening sequence. The door slid silently open and the guard, unsure of the situation, peered cautiously into the room, lining his gun on Delta Ten who was lounging unconcerned on one of the beds.

"Where's the other…" he began, and Raan answered his question by grabbing the rifle by it's barrel and swinging it around. The guard hurtled into the room, letting go of the weapon at just the right moment to slam against the wall where Raan gave him a sharp rap with his own gun butt.

"Let's go," snapped Raan, poking his head out into the corridor. Delta Ten locked the guard in his own cell and they set off purposely as if they knew where they were going.

"We must find Major Erion," said Del quietly.

"Sure," answered Raan, but first we have to set this place to blow. I finally figured out what this guy is up to and we have to stop him."

"My first priority is the safety of Major Erion." stated the robot stoically. Raan grabbed Delta Ten's arm and turned the robot to face him. "Del, I need your help to blow this place."

"I must see to the safety of Major Erion."

"Listen, we are standing in a massive arms factory. Dolton Blass has started this war for his own ends. Don't you see, there aren't any hi tech survivors from Serrell. They're all Blass's people. Work it out; our lives against thousands that could die in this phoney war." The robot still looked unconvinced but Raan persisted. "Look, Blass is supplying the Marine Corps with arms now he has the franchise. He's engineered this war and he's making a fortune on Aurian lives. We must stop him; Erion would want us to." The stoic android carefully weighed the pros and cons. His intricate programming was very delicately balanced where human lives were concerned and Erion was first on his list of priorities. Raan hoped he had put the case strongly enough with sending the robot over the edge.

"Affirmative," he said at last. "We must stop Dolton Blass from manufacturing more arms."

"Great!" snapped Raan. "Now, where's the main power source?"

"Deep below us." answered Delta Ten. "It is a plasma reactor."

"Let's get down there," said Raan, heading for the nearest aircar. They had taken the guard's pass, which had a high priority rating and the aircar doors soon opened into the outer room that housed the blast proof doors of the reactor. White suited technicians were busy at computers all round the room, and were so engrossed in their work that it was some seconds before anyone noticed them. A woman shouted and raised her hand to the red alarm button, but Raan fired a bolt from the guard's rifle into the air which stopped everyone cold.

"Get over there, all of you," snapped Raan. The eight or so techs were herded to a corner of the room and waited to see would happen next. Raan called to Delta Ten. "Can you do it?"

"We are in the computer room that controls the cooling system for the reactor," he answered slowly, checking the monitors on the console. "If we can shut the computer down, it will overheat and explode."

"He's going to kill us all," wailed a woman, twisting out of her colleagues grip and running towards Raan. "You can't do this!"

"How many people do you think you've killed so far?" asked Raan softly. The woman opened her mouth to deny it, but Raan spoke first. "Didn't think a few dead 'Terrys' and a couple of Marines mattered did you? Didn't occur to you that they had friends and families, or if it did, you didn't care." He pushed the woman back to her waiting colleagues. "You make me sick." Raan turned his head to watch Delta Ten at a console. "How's it coming?" A klaxon started up and Raan guessed that someone must have found the guard in their cell or Erion was up to something on her own. "Hurry it up Del," he called, swivelling his gaze back to his prisoners. "We're running out of time." Delta Ten had the front off the console and dug around inside it. He pulled out a group of circuits on a board and the lights dimmed momentarily.

"It is done," he said simply. "The cooling system is now inoperative." A second klaxon started up, adding to the din.

Delta Ten walked to another console and started to pull the front of it as well.

"What are you doing now?"

"The back up system must also be incapacitated." he explained. By the looks on the faces of the technicians, their worst nightmare was about to begin and Raan guessed that there were no more fail safes.

"All right," began Raan. "This place is going to blow. I suggest you all get the hell out." There was a concerted rush or the door and within a few seconds, Raan and Del were alone. "How long have we got before it blows?" asked Raan.

"Thirty minutes, no more. I suggest we find Erion and make good our escape," answered the calm faced android. As they ran out into the corridor, a computerised woman's voice began to speak.

"Warning! The plasma generator cooling system has malfunctioned. The reactor will destruct in twenty eight minutes from now. Warning! The plasma generator cooling system has malfunctioned..." It droned sweetly on, oblivious to the panic it was causing. Everyone had the same idea. Escape! Fights and scuffles were breaking out around the air car doors as people rushed towards the exits.

"Which way now?" yelled Raan above the din, as they reached an intersection.

"This way," stated Delta Ten, walking briskly around the corner. Raan tried to reach Erion again on his wrist com-link, with no reply. He was becoming increasingly worried about her and broke into a run, thumping Delta Ten on the arm as he passed him.

"Come on Del, lets hurry it up; we haven't much time."

"We have twenty one minutes and forty two seconds," he pointed out.

"Forget the countdown Del, let's just find Erion and get the hell out of here."

On the other side of the complex, Erion had been sitting opposite Dolton Blass, watching the piggy man stuff large amounts of food into his mouth and swill it down with expensive wine. He talked as he ate, boasting proudly about his achievements.

"We built this place two years ago and brought the staff here to run it. We have been planning this for a long time, my dear. I was going to ask you to stay here and share it all with me, but somehow I don't think you would be very loyal."

"Everyone has their price," said Erion, playing for time.

"You could not forgive the death of your friends, my dear. No, I'm afraid you are going to have to go." The door opened and the hard faced secretary came in to the room.

"Sir, the two men have escaped."

"What?" bellowed Dolton Blass, tearing the napkin from his throat as he rose from the table. "Sound the alarm. They must be found and killed on sight. Do you understand? Kill them!" He turned to Erion as the woman rushed out. "What are their plans?" Almost immediately, a second alarm sounded. "The reactor!" yelled Blass. "They've set it to blow," he launched himself at Erion, his strong fat hands reaching for her throat. "You little bitch. Tell me who you are!"

Although she could feel herself blacking out, Erion resisted the urge to try and remove Blass's hands from her throat. Instead, she reached under her dress for a little dagger that was strapped to her thigh. Starfire had given her the idea of carrying a concealed weapon and Delta Ten had made this one for her. It was a little crude and not very powerful, but the hard plastic it was made from did not show up on weapon scans. Dolton Blass testified to it's effectiveness a second later when Erion activated the laser blade and plunged deep it into his back. He reared up with a scream and fell sideways, landing on the table and sending everything crashing to the floor. Erion was off in a sprint for the door. She opened the door and almost made it. The wall cracked by her head and she stopped in the doorway and raised her hands, knowing the uncomfortable sound of a nearby laser bolt strike. She turned slowly to see Dolton Blass standing about ten feet from her. He was weaving and swaying, but held a wicked little plasma bolt pistol in his fat hand that drew a bead on her heart that never wavered. Erion tensed for a sidelong dive that would take her out of it's line of fire, but she knew her chances of making it were not great. The fat man's eyes were glazing and she knew only the desire to kill her was keeping him alive. With a visible effort, he tightened his finger on the trigger and snarled, "Bitch!"

CHAPTER 10

"Starfire, Wake up!" The voice seemed to come from far away. Hal shook her, gently. She opened her eyes and tried to focus on the shape above her. Her vision cleared and she blinked and tried to sit up.

"Hal," she croaked. "What happened?" She accepted a drink of water front him and eased herself into a sitting position on the couch where she had been lying. "I remember now; the village!" She cast a look around her. "Every time I wake up I'm in a different place. Where are we now?" Hal shrugged,

"I don't know," he said "I woke up here too. I know there isn't a way out. Not even a door!"

"Great!" muttered Starfire to herself as she studied the room in more detail. It was square, shiny and black, and apart from a couch and a small table there was nothing else to be seen. The furniture looked like it had been moulded from the same material as the walls, for it rose seamlessly out of the floor. There were no doors or windows and no visible light source, although the room was not dark.

Starfire handed the tumbler back to Hal and tried to stand but her senses reeled and Hal grabbed her arm to steady her.

"Wow!" she gasped, sitting down again, "That gas is strong stuff. I wonder how long we've been out?" Hal raised his arm to look at his com link and stared in surprise at his unmarked wrists."

"Look," he said to Starfire, holding his hands out to her. "Someone's fixed them up."

"It's incredible" she gasped "There isn't any scarring." Hal shrugged and sat by her on the couch.

"I figure we've only been out for fifteen minutes or so. I saw you were out cold and I tried to find a way out of this place."

"Are we in a prison then?" asked Starfire. The wall in front of them suddenly glowed brightly and disappeared. They stood up, reaching for weapons that were not there as a short, smiling Terrellian woman suddenly appeared in front of them. Both her arms held out in an unmistakable gesture of friendship and they could see that she only had three fingers on each hand.

"Welcome," she beamed. "I hope you are both recovered. The gas is powerful but the effects soon wear off." She spoke Terrellian, but in a way that suggested it was not her first language.

"What the hell…" began Hal,

"Where are we?" asked Starfire.

"I'm sure you have many questions," began the woman, "and if you come with me, they will all be answered." She stepped backwards and beckoned them to follow. With nothing to loose, they walked after her.

The woman waved her hand and the opening disappeared behind them, leaving a grey flat wall.

"Come along!" She hastened them along like naughty

children as they both stared at it. They walked quickly behind her into a wide street. It was obvious they were underground, but the ceiling was far above them, and trees grew on every corner. Fountains sparkled in the centre of café lined squares and smiling people went about their business, calling greetings to the woman and nodding courteously at Hal and Starfire. "Not far now," she breezed, turning a corner. The atmosphere changed slightly although the street furniture was the same. Now people bustled along with purpose, some carrying portable data packs. It was clear they were now in some sort of work area. The woman stopped at a blank wall. "Here we are," she waved her hand and the wall disappeared. "In you go." This room was furnished much like the other and they walked straight in, the wall closing behind them. Two loungers sat in the centre of the room and Starfire took one but Hal preferred to stand behind her.

"Welcome!" boomed a deep, pleasant male tenor voice. "Please make yourselves comfortable. I'm sure you have many questions to ask, but first, I would like you to watch something." The wall in front of them lit up to show a life size holo movie of themselves from the moment they landed on Serrell. It was speeded up a little in places, and the boring bits were missed out. It ended with Hal and Starfire at the sacrificial stone.

"Very entertaining." said Hal, dryly.

"I thought it was very good," said Starfire, "Especially my bit."

"We have shown you this to prove to you that what you see is really happening. We have more for you to see and it concerns your friends."

"Play it," grunted Hal. They watched, enthralled at the scenes that rolled into view. The holo showed Keen appearing at the clearing and faded at the point when the last troop carrier entered the cliff face.

"We cannot show you more," The voice was apologetic. "The force field was erected as soon as the last car went in. I must inform you though, that your friends are probably in deadly peril."

"Why doesn't that surprise me?" muttered Starfire.

"I've seen that man before," began Hal. "The one who called himself Keen, but I'm sure that wasn't his name."

"He works for this man," said the voice. A holo picture lit up to show the waddling form of Dolton Blass. Starfire's mouth dropped open, and she looked back at Hal. His knuckles were white as he gripped the back of the chair, but otherwise showed no emotion.

"How old is that recording?" he growled.

"Ten point four of your hours," answered the voice.

"His name is Dolton Blass." said Hal softly, "I thought he was dead."

"Oh he isn't dead," continued the voice. "He built that underground complex to make warships and weapons. He is supplying both to Auria and Terrell."

"I don't understand." said Starfire.

"He started the war," said Hal flatly. He's using his own pilots to raid Terrell, then he supplied the Terrellians with arms to defend themselves. I've seen him do the same thing before, only not on such a large scale as this."

"You are correct, Terrellian," said the voice. Hal squeezed Starfire's shoulder.

"If he's got Erion and Raan, they're in big trouble."

"What can we do from here?" asked Starfire, "I don't even know where here is."

"We can get you into the complex," put in the voice.

"What do you want in return?" asked Hal.

"We want you to put an and to this evil on our planet, and stop Dolton Blass," said the disembodied voice.

"Why don't you do it yourselves?" asked Hal in a hard voice.

"We have no weapons, Terrellian, nor do we need them. We abhor violence."

"Sure," sneered Hal. "But just this once, for the good of the community, you'll hire someone to do it for you." He walked forward to face the brightly lit screen. "Your sort make me sick. In your own way you're just as bad as Dolton." There was a long silence and Starfire left her seat to stand by his side.

"Terrellian, your ship is damaged. Our technicians say it cannot be made space worthy without special equipment which you do not have."

"Is he right?" whispered Hal out of the corner of his mouth. Starfire nodded.

"I'd say 'damaged' was one hell of an understatement," she whispered back. "It's a wreck!"

"In return for your help," began the voice, "We will refuel your ship and make it space worthy." Hal shook his head.

"I don't make deals with folks who won't show themselves." Starfire looked quickly at him.

"Hal, what are you doing?" There was another long silence then a tunnel lit up in front of them, leading slightly downwards and to the left. "Oh, well done!" she gritted.

"You don't have to come," he said softly, heading for the opening.

"You don't think I'm staying here on my own do you?" she retorted, rushing to keep up with him. They walked steadily in a downward spiral for several minutes, conscious that the narrow tunnel was closing behind them. It was not a place to be if you were agoraphobic, but that never bothered native Terrellians. They turned a corner and found themselves in a dark, circular room. Large vague shapes loomed around the outside of it, dimly visible in the gloom. The room suddenly lit up and Starfire gasped, grabbing Hal's arm in a sudden panic. Even his nerves were not that strong, but apart from an involuntary start, he made no sound and stood looking up at the dozen creatures defiantly. They were beings from a nightmare; at least eight feet tall and not even vaguely humanoid. They were dragons. One was taller than the rest, and he raised a blackened claw towards them.

"Please come forward," The warm, kind voice was the same but it didn't seem to match it's owner somehow. His head was birdlike, with shiny red eyes and a long reptilian jaw, glinting with several rows of thorny teeth. Dark grey leathery wings folded behind its back, ending with a black shiny spur. Stubby, scaled legs ended in birdlike feet tipped with wicked looking talons. These gripped a dull metal perch a foot off the floor. It unfurled one wing and motioned them forward. "You are not repulsed by our presence?" It seemed surprised.

"Why should we be?" asked Hal, dragging Starfire forward with him. "Star, come say hello."

"Hi!" she smiled weakly, raising a hand and wiggling her fingers in salute. Hal and Starfire shared a look. They could quite clearly hear the voices of the dragons, but they were not using their mouths to speak.

"I do not understand," another of the creatures spoke. "The villagers are terrified of us."

"The galaxy is a big place," began Starfire. "It's full of different species. It's just that you took us by surprise."

"We meant to, Terrellian," said the obvious leader. "I wanted to see what you were made of."

"And you saw," snarled Hal, "Now if you've had your fun, let's get down to business. What do you want us to do?"

"Why are you so angry?" asked a smaller creature, tipping its head on one side in curiosity. Hal stiffened and Starfire said quickly.

"Where we come from, it is considered impolite to question strangers about their personal feelings."

"As it is among us," said the leader. He fixed the younger creature with a red eyed stare that made it look down at its claws. "You must forgive my son. As you have probably guessed, we are telepathic but you are the first non Trenee he has ever been able to converse with directly. Prince Grennig has let his curiosity get the better of him and scanned deeper than he should. Please forgive him this transgression." Hal nodded quickly and Starfire continued,

"Who are the people in your city then? Have they always been here?"

"The people you see in our complex are descendants of the few colonists we managed to save many years ago. They have never seen us and we communicate through audio only."

"What about the savages outside?" asked Starfire,

"They are also descendants of the Terrellian colonists. We try to help them as much as we can, although they are mutants as you have seen, some of them little more than troglodytes."

"Do you know what happened to them?" asked Starfire.

"They were foolish and tried to build a weapon with equipment that was supposed to help them survive," answered another creature. "It bode well for the Trenee that we were already in hiding from them down here or we would have suffered their fate. They started to argue amongst themselves and a battle was fought. There was an explosion but we saved as many as we could. Some survived the blast but were mutated by the radiation. We watch over them and help them as best we can."

"In the hut," snapped Hal suddenly, "Just before I passed out I saw something."

"One of our drone cameras, Terrellian. The villagers have learned not to touch it and it does them no harm."

"But why the sacrifice?" asked Starfire. "It was pretty scary you know."

"My apologies young one, but the stone is the way we bring people down from the surface. There is no way we would have let you come to harm. Sometimes normal children are born to these people. We take them in the sacrificial ritual and bring them down here to live in our city. The savages are well rewarded and are only too pleased to comply. Alas, they also send down anyone who falls from grace with their leader. In your case however, we are more than pleased."

"I'm kinda pleased about it myself," muttered Hal under his breath.

"Have you been on this planet a long time?" asked Starfire.

"The Trenee have lived here in secret for over ten thousand years," The tall one drew himself up proudly. "Once, we were too many to count, now just a few thousand remain. Please, let me introduce myself. I am Kaura, leader of The Trenee. These people are my governors, and this," he motioned proudly with one wing, "is Prince Grennig, my son and heir to my throne." The smaller Trenee, and he topped six and a half feet, stepped forward, moving awkwardly on his birdlike feet. He held their weapons in his claw tipped wings and he handed them to Hal and Starfire.

"I was watching you," he said quickly to Hal. "You're really fast with that pistol. And in the hut when you were outnumbered…" He motioned a fast draw with an imaginary gun.

"Grennig!" warned Kaura. The young prince bowed.

"I'm sorry, father." He turned to Hal "My apologies, sir." Hal smiled grimly.

"Listen to your father, Prince Grennig. Being fast with a gun is a sure way to get yourself killed. I've seen too many friends die who thought they were the best."

"But…"

"That's enough, Grennig. I have let you stand in on this meeting as a personal boon, now please be silent." He turned to face Hal. "Will you help us?"

"Sure," said Hal, buckling on his gun belt and seating the big pistol correctly, "If you'll fix up our ship."

"It will be done," answered Kaura. He glided from his podium as if he was on wires to land beside them and motioned to the wall with a claw tipped wing. Another tunnel opened up in front of them. It was well lit, straight and went as far as the eye could see. A small, bullet shaped hover car sat at its entrance. Kaura and Grennig walked with them towards it.

"Good luck," said Grennig. "I wish I was coming with you."

"The tunnel will seal behind you," began Kaura. He seemed to want to say more, gathered his wits, and continued. "We are a shy people and value our privacy. We do not wish others to know we are here. Since Dolton Blass came here we have not even dared visit the surface in case we are seen."

"If that's the way you want it," said Hal softly, "No one will hear about you through us."

"We are grateful." Kaura bowed and they bowed back before

climbing into the car. It set off as soon as they were seated and Starfire risked a backward glance to see young Grennig standing alone, one wing raised in silent salute.

CHAPTER 11

Starfire and Hal sat in the speeding shuttle car, the sides of the tunnel blurring into white streaks as they hurtled onwards. They covered more than thirty kliks in only a few minutes, then the little car slowed quickly to emerge in a windowless room filled with pipes and tubes.

"Where do you think we are?" asked Starfire, looking around.

"Now where did I put my map." answered Hal dryly, patting imaginary pockets.

"Oh, come on!" snapped Starfire. There were two exits from the room and they tossed a credit to see which one to take. Their choice made, they set off, not seeing the little shuttle reverse back down it's tunnel and the walls close in behind it.

"Look," said Starfire, pointing. "An aircar; let's try it." The programming panel looked familiar, and with the uncanny knack of a flight console operator, Starfire took a lucky guess and pressed a few buttons at random, bringing them out near the command centre. As they opened the doors and stepped quickly outside, a siren sounded. People had started to fill the corridors, rising panic making them run.

"I hate sirens," moaned Starfire. "It always means bad news somewhere along the line."

"They're in a hell of a hurry to get away, that's for sure." mused Hal. "Come on, we'll follow them." A second siren started up and a helpful computer informed them that they only had eighteen minutes to clear the complex before they were blown to bits. "Looks like Raan beat us to it," said Hal with a wicked grin.

"Then let's find the others and get out of here," panted Starfire. They stopped at an aircar terminal where a fight was taking place as too many people tried to cram into the little shuttle. Hal grabbed one, shoving his gun barrel up the man's nose.

"Where do we find Dolton Blass?" he asked. The computer spoke again.

"Seventeen minutes and counting…"

"Gotta get out!" screamed the man, trying to pull out of Hal's grasp.

"Dolton Blass!" snapped Hal again, "Where is he?"

"He'll be in his office if he's not already out of here."

"Where would that be?" asked Hal gently, stroking the man's cheek with his gun barrel.

"Follow the red line," yelled the man, twisting out of Hal's grasp to pound on the now closed aircar doors.

"Follow the red line?" echoed Starfire. Hal tapped her arm and pointed downwards. Several different coloured lines were painted on the floor. They picked out the red one and started running in the direction of the small arrows on it. Two minutes later, they stood outside the double office doors where the red lines and arrows converged. Hal opened them quickly and stepped inside to be confronted by Vander, who stood behind her desk. She had swapped her pistol for a rifle, which was aimed at Hal's chest. She sneered at him with obvious contempt.

"Halt or I fire, Terrellian." It was very clear that she would rather shoot than not, and Hal stood quietly, his arms by his sides.

"Lady, I haven't time to argue," he said softly. "Put the rifle down and get the hell out of here alive."

"Unbuckle that gun belt, 'Terry' and you...." Vander motioned to Starfire with the rifle, "Drop..." Hal shot her through the heart as soon as the rifle's muzzle moved away from him. Starfire, who had been watching Vander, was dumbstruck. She had thought Raan was fast with a gun, but there was no comparison with Hal. She had not seen his hand move, but Vander was dead, sitting on the floor with her back against the wall and her chest a mask of blood.

"See you're quiet for once," he murmured as he strode past her to the connecting doors. He triggered the mechanism and they opened to reveal Erion framed in the far doorway, a split second away from death. Hal went into action again and shot Blass in the right shoulder. His body was mostly hidden by Erion, and it was the only target he could safely hit with out endangering her. Blass screamed and spun around, the gun falling from his hand. Erion dived aside and Hal shot again, hitting Blass in the head and killing him instantly. His corpse jerked from the blast to lie on its stomach a few feet away.

"Hal!" she gasped from the doorway, staring across at him in disbelief. "I thought I'd had it there." Hal reached down and deactivated the little knife in Blass's back. The hilt fell neatly into his hand and he passed it to Erion, brushing aside her thanks.

"I'd say he's really dead this time," said Starfire, looking down at the body.

"Yep!" answered Hal, "If it really is him."

"Oh come on," began Starfire, "How many idiots that look like Dolton Blass could there be in the universe."

"Hey you guys," shouted a voice. "Come on, we have to get out of this place, It's gonna blow."

"In twelve minutes and forty six seconds," added Delta Ten.

"Raan, Del!" they grinned at one another like idiots for a moment, then Hal said,

"We have to get to the surface."

"Blass's personal aircar is through here," stated Erion. "It has priority one." They all piled in and Erion said, "Can you hotwire it, Del?"

"Yes, Erion," answered the android, his long brown fingers poised over the numeric pad. They were soon moving and two minutes later they stepped out at the hover park in the tunnel entrance.

"There's the truck!" called Raan, "Come on!" They rushed over to it and Delta Ten opened the hatch. Raan quickly fired up the engines and pulled the heavy vehicle out into the stream of traffic, pushing smaller cars out of the way. The hover cars were faster, and many overtook the cumbersome ATV, but they were out into the bright sunlight with minutes to spare. They surged forward at full speed then Raan stopped the truck with seconds to go.

"We'll need full shields," stated Delta Ten, firing the emergency anchors into the ground.

"Three...Two...One!" he called switching on the aft scanner. They all watched but nothing happened for a few seconds, then the ground shook underneath them and they grasped their seats for support. Smoke poured from the tunnel entrance and several muffled explosions could be heard. Suddenly, the sky lit up and their scanner whited out. The temperature alarm shot off the scale for a split second then died down to a safe level and it was over. When the dust cleared, they could see that the cliff had collapsed over the tunnel entrance. If there was anything left inside, it was sealed forever.

"Del, scan for life signs," ordered Erion.

"There are no signs from the complex," he began, "but there are eighty nine survivors on the surface."

"The Marines will pick them up," began Erion. "Now the place is blown, the shield will be down." They digested this fact for a moment then Starfire said,

"Well, we've done what we were sent to do. Let's go before they get here."

"In what, Star," began Raan. "Our ship is one long dent in the sand." Starfire grinned at Hal.

"We know something you don't know."

"Oh come on Lieutenant, I'm not in the mood for games," said Erion wearily.

"Just head for the ship, Del," began Starfire, "and hope we reach it before the Marines get here. The General might not have had the time to tell them we're the good guys after all."

"Ship ahead," stated the robot, pulling the truck over to one side.

"Is it ours?" asked Erion.

"Sure," answered Starfire.

"But we shouldn't reach it for another day at least." She caught Hal's eye and he shrugged.

"Is this what you know that we don't?" asked Raan.

"Not exactly," began Starfire as they alighted from the ATV. "Let's take a look at her." Delta Ten was already at the stern of the massive ship, checking her engines with a portable scanner. Apart from some laser scorching he proclaimed them functional. Starfire and Raan opened a new rear ramp and went inside and up to the pilot section to check the controls. Hal stowed away the ATV and joined them to check over the defence systems, his sixth sense telling him they would soon be needed.

"Is she space worthy?" asked Erion,

"All systems check out," answered Starfire." She's fully fuelled and ready to go."

"How long till you can take off, Lieutenant?"

"About five minutes to power up, but there may be some minor malfunctions sort out."

"She means bypass the fail safes," explained Raan.

"I do not," she said with a guilty look. "That's illegal. Anyway, I wouldn't know how!"

"While you're on pre flight, will you pass me the hand-link?" asked Erion. "I'd like to contact my father and make sure we have a safe passage back home." She took the hand held link and tapped out her father's code on the small console in the handle. Static was all she could receive. "I can't get through," she muttered.

"Perhaps the link is out." suggested Raan, running a quick check. "No, it's okay. The shield is down and there's no ionic interference. There's no one at the other end to receive."

"That can't be," snapped Erion. "Father wouldn't abandon us. We had everything planned to the last detail. He's been keeping a channel open since we left. I'll go through the ship's main systems." She leaned past Starfire and entered the code into the ship's communication post. The light stayed resolutely red and she quickly tried again, entering the wrong code in her haste.

"Take it easy," murmured Raan, gently disengaging her from the equipment and sitting her down at her navigation post. "Perhaps he's not at home right now."

"He's probably dead!" grunted Hal from his seat opposite her.

"Damn it Hal, do you have to say it like that?" gritted Raan.

"There's no other way to say it." he answered, matching Erion's shocked gaze without flinching.

"He's right," she said, miserably. "Father wouldn't desert us."

"Maybe..." began Starfire.

"Face facts, Starfire," cut in Hal. "This thing is bigger and dirtier than we all thought. Someone pretty high up on both sides must be involved."

"Yeah, and don't forget that attack by Captain Ryan's patrol," put in Raan. "Somebody ordered it. Maybe they found our what the General was up to. He didn't actually go through the official chain of command, did he?"

"Even if that was so, he would only face an enquiry," answered Erion. "The raids have stopped after all. He could be under house arrest." She sighed deeply. "If only I knew for sure." She looked at the faces around her. "You can understand that, can't you?"

"Sure," answered Raan, "Only we don't know if the General had time to clear our names. There's probably a price on our heads now and we wouldn't get past the outer marker before we were blasted out of space."

"What about the High Commander," began Starfire. "Couldn't we contact him?"

"He could be anywhere in the galaxy," said Erion. "We must think! Isn't there anyone on Terrell we can trust? Raan, even you must have one friend."

"Thanks very much," answered Raan then he caught Starfire's eye and they said together.

"Cully!" Raan leaned across the console and tapped out Cully's personal code. At the second attempt, his wheedling tones filled the pilot section.

"Yeah, this is sanitation engineer third class Cully speaking. What do yer want?"

"Cully, it's me, Raan,"

"Oh, hi there Cap. They says you was a traitor, you know. Me, I says no way! You was always good to me, Cap."

"Never mind that now, Cully. I need some information."

"I don't know, Cap There's a warning out about you."

"I know that Cully. I'll transfer by computer."

"I like cash, Captain, you know that. Good old fashioned creds."

"Cully, I tell you what I'll do. You tell me what I want to know and I'll transfer you a hundred."

"I'll have to pay tax if we go through he computer."

"All right, god dammit, I'll pay the tax as well!"

"Okay Cap, Here's my number." They all waited while Raan patiently tapped out his own personal computer number, his central bank number, Cully's number, and finally the amount to be transferred. The system was designed so that anyone could use it and many fail safes were built into the programming. There was a short delay, then a big green 'ok' lit up Starfire's screen together with the standing charge for the transaction.

"You got that, Cully?"

"Sure Cap. Now, what do you want to know?"

"Do you know where General Dubois is?"

"The old man?" whined Cully, "He bought it!" Erion closed her eyes and sat back in her seat.

"How?" grunted Hal.

"How'd he die?" repeated Raan.

"Aircar accident." answered Cully. "First one here for fifty years or more. Funny, you think you're safe in those things, then whammo! Yer brake's fail and down yer go!"

"All right, Cully, that's enough. Is there anything else you can tell us?"

"Everything's going crazy down here, Cap. There's talk of changes in the whole Federation. You see, the old man weren't alone; The High Commander was in there with him."

"Commander Nooran?" asked Raan, just to make sure.

"The very same."

"Dead?" just to make absolutely sure.

"When yer aircar falls from the eightieth level, there ain't much to scrape off the walls, Cap."

"The only two people who could have cleared us," said Starfire softly.

"Who's taken over?" asked Raan. "The Admiral of the Fleet?"

"No. Some guy on the Federation Council called Roland," grumbled Cully, his tone indicating his dislike. "He's already made a lotta changes."

"Changes?" asked Raan, "Like what?"

"Hold it, Cap," began Cully. "Someone at the door." They dimly heard footsteps walking away from them, together with Cully's fading voice whining, "All right, all right, I'm coming." Starfire caught Raan's eye, a strange foreboding clutching at her. The pilot section filled with the sound of laser fire and Hal leaned forward to shut off the link.

"What the hell?" muttered Raan.

"Your friend's dead!" snapped Hal. "They were listening."

"Who was listening?" asked Erion.

"Repeaters." explained Hal. "Hi-res laser repeating rifles, Standard Galactic Police issue. Only they can afford to waste ammo like that."

"Poor Cully," muttered Starfire. "I can't understand why the Police would be bothered about him. He was small fry."

"They must have traced the credit transfer," began Hal. "They'll know where we are."

"Hal's right," said Erion, pulling herself together. "We have to get off this planet before they send up their fighters. Fire her up Lieutenant, and lets go!"

CHAPTER 12

Starfire looked up dubiously from her controls. "I think this thing is space worthy, but I wouldn't like to take it into combat," she warned.

"It's that or fight from here." said Hal.

"He's right," put in Erion. "It's better than no chance at all."

"All right," answered Starfire, making her pre-flight checks. "Raan, give me a hand here."

"You got it," he said, sliding into the co pilot seat. Erion and Hal made ready at their stations and Delta Ten returned from the rear of the ship where he had been checking the replacement hatch.

"Everything is in order," he said calmly. "We are space worthy."

"Just as well," put in Hal. "We were going anyway." Delta Ten ignored him and turned to face Erion.

"I heard your communication with Terrell," he began. "Your father gave me certain instructions before we left for this planet.

In the event of his death, should you and Hal survive, I was to ask Mr Hal to take you to Thirty-Seven's Place."

"Thirty Seven's Place?" asked Erion. "What's that?"

"I know it." admitted the gunman with a rare grin. "I didn't know the General knew about it though. It's in the Keloran sector." He leaned over Erion's shoulder and punched the co-ordinates into her computer. "Okay Pilot Five." he said to Starfire. "Your course is plotted."

"And laid in," added Erion, making minute adjustments. "I have a green light on the course," stated Raan, locking it into his own computer."

"Start up sequence is initiated." called Starfire. A low whine started and Raan called,

"Start up sequence running. No malfunctions."

"So far so good," muttered Starfire. "Let's try for ignition."

"A-One for ignition," confirmed Raan. Although the sound proof cladding had been restored, they could feel the throbbing power of the two massive engines as they thundered into life. Starfire slowly pushed forward the two throttle levers and the ship began to rise out of the desert on it's manoeuvring thrusters. Their vision was obscured by clouds of sand, but as the ship rose higher the sand thinned out until finally, the blowers on the vision port cleared it away. As soon as they had enough lift, Starfire brought the main engines into play and gently lifted the nose of the gigantic machine. It rose high into the air and through the wispy clouds.

"Scan for fighters, Del." ordered Erion.

"None at present..." answered the robot. The pale blue of the Serrellian sky gave way to the inky blackness of space and Starfire slowly turned the ship onto its new heading.

"Can't say I'm sorry to leave that place," she confided to Raan.

"How's the ship?" he asked, conscious of the creaking and groaning sounds of metal somewhere far beneath them in the empty hold.

"Sluggish," she answered, not taking her eyes off the controls. "How's our power?"

"Eighty per cent."

"That's just great!" she said dryly." We can't make the jump. It'll have to be the long way round folks."

"And how long is that?" asked Hal, checking out the combat computers.

"At this speed, thirteen months and four days." answered Erion. No one spoke but they glared at one other.

"We really need to make some repairs." said Raan.

"You can drop me off at the nearest class M planet." stated Hal, flatly.

"Fighters at extreme range, in battle configuration." stated Delta Ten from his scanning post. Raan left his seat at Starfire's side.

"Take over Del," he shouldered his way past the robot, muttering, "Thirteen months and four days. I'll go mad."

"That is if we survive this," pointed out Starfire.

"That's what we need, Lieutenant, a positive attitude." said Erion.

"Combat computers are on line and we have telemetry." called Raan as he brought up the heads up display.

"That's something anyway," muttered Starfire. She caught Hal's eye. "You're going to have to take out all the opposition. We can't outrun them."

"Forget the rules, Star," he said grimly,. "We'll play this Terrellian style."

"What's that?" asked Erion

"Every dirty trick in the book," snarled Raan.

"You got it!" grinned Starfire.

"Fighters in range," stated Delta Ten. "Wasp Fighters, Class Six."

"Galactic Police ships," said Erion. "Well at least they're not Marines."

"You mean I can shoot to kill, Major?" sneered Hal.

"Very funny, killer," she snapped at him. "Just do what you're best at." The communications alarm sounded and Raan put it through the ship's systems so they could all hear.

"Space freighter Madillion, this is Commander Fee of the New Federation Galactic Police, Gamma Squadron. You will lower your shields and prepare to be boarded."

"Go to hell!" snapped Raan,

"Then we will blow you out of the sky." The commander cut the link and Raan shrugged.

"Here they come," called Erion. "Fire when ready." Seven small, one seater ships converged on them, splitting up as they passed Madillion and firing on it as they went by in a classic attack plan. Hal and Starfire were ready for them and she swung the ship around as he fired, giving him a wider arc of fire. Erion and Raan exchanged looks. They were both used to flying in combat and although this looked unorthodox, it seemed to be working. Hal took out two fighters in the first pass, Raan missed one fighter, but scored a glancing blow on another, forcing it to withdraw.

"Too easy," muttered Hal under his breath. He couldn't have known it, but Fee's troop was newly formed with young recruits. They fought in a classic, text book way which the experienced crew on Madillion unconsciously predicted and countered with ruthless efficiency. The remaining four ships split up and dived at Madillion, scoring several hits on the already damaged shields. Starfire forced the huge ship across the heavens like a demented insect while Hal and Raan took shots at every fighter that crossed their path. They were slowly winning, but the freighter had not been built to take such a pounding and was beginning to show the strain.

"We're losing shields," called out Erion, worriedly. The ship rocked violently as it took another hit.

"Damn it, Star," snapped Hal as the freighter dipped suddenly and he missed his shot.

"I must protect that port shield. It's failing. Erion, can you give me more speed?"

"The power pack's draining," she answered. "Del, see what you can do with it."

"The fault does not lie within the ship's controls," said Delta Ten, calmly. "The power converter has polarised."

"What the hell does that mean?" yelled Starfire. "Can you fix it or not?"

"Not in flight," answered the robot, "We must land or dock."

"Well somebody had better do something," muttered Starfire as the ship took another hit. There was only one working fighter left now and it was evading all their attempts to destroy it.

"This guy is good," murmured Hal, more to himself than anyone else. "Star, he's coming in close. Keep her steady." His grey eyes squinted into the firing grid and his long fingers almost caressed the firing controls. The fighter passed them, executed a perfect rolling dive and fired on the already weakened port shield. It buckled and collapsed, forcing Madillion to roll over with the impact. The gyros screamed against the strain but Starfire and Erion managed to turn the ship around so that the unshielded quarter was away from the little fighter. Delta Ten was busy with his fire extinguisher, fighting a losing battle against many short circuit flare ups. The pilot section took on an eerie, red hue as the lighting failed completely and the multi coloured reflections from the controls and screens seemed to drift with the acrid smoke oozing from some of the panels.

"He's coming in for another pass." said Raan, wiping tears from his smoke filled eyes.

"The starboard engine's gone," began Starfire quietly. "I can't turn in time,"

"Hal?" asked Erion. She looked into the flat hopelessness of Hal's face for her answer.

"He knows we're a sitting duck," growled Raan. "He's taking his time."

"Ram him, Lieutenant." stated Erion.

"It's the only way we can take him out." warned Hal. "Starfire, give it all you have. Straight at him!" Starfire pushed the throttles forward and the mighty freighter wobbled its way towards the galactic fighter.

"All power to the front shields," she ordered, sounding a lot braver than she felt.

"It's crazy," began Raan, 'But I like it." The fighter was firing short busts at the ship, each one weakening the shield a little more.

"He's low on power himself," explained Hal. "He has to come in closer to finish us off."

"This is it!" called Raan as the little ship hurtled straight towards them. Time seemed to slow and all eyes were fixed on the fighter headed straight for them. There was a slight jolt, then nothing. Starfire peered through her fingers.

"We're still here. What happened?"

"Don't ask me. One second it was there, the next it was gone." answered Erion. Raan was on the scanner, looking for the fighter.

"It's gone!" he shouted. "There's nothing here. Wait a minute, floating debris; frozen water particles; it must have blown up. Hey, I have another ion trail."

"Another ship?" asked Erion. "Where is it then?"

"There was another ship," began Delta Ten. He shouldered his way to the front and pressed the forward scanner recap. He re-started it at a quarter speed then slowed it to frame by frame, stopping it at the vital moment. A grey blur had forced its way in between the two converging ships. At the same time, the attacking fighter seemed to be expanding at the seams. Delta Ten advanced another frame and the grey blur had gone. The fighter seemed to be moving away from them still in the process of blowing up.

"You saw that?" asked Raan. "What was it?"

"A twin seater planet hopper, I believe." answered the stoic robot. "It was of alien design and travelling at light point nine nine six."

"That's impossible," snapped Starfire.

"It returns," stated Delta Ten quietly. "See for yourself." Madillion lurched again and any instrumentation that was working glowed red for an instant before settling down again. Then it was there. One second space was empty, the next, a sleek black planet hopper sat in front of them, matching their drift and appearing motionless to them. It was dangerously close. So close that they could see the outline of the pilot in his brightly lit cockpit.

"Incredible," gasped Starfire, "How could he have sustained light point nine like that without the space distortion blowing him to bits?"

"Because he's flying an alien ship – and he's crazy," answered Hal. "His name is Con Tranter."

"You know this man?" asked Erion. The names were star fields visible from Terrell. "Is he Terrellian?"

"Sort of," muttered Hal.

"Hey in there!" called a voice, showing no regard for standard space recognition courtesies. Erion leaned forward and took the hand link from its slot on the console.

"This is commercial space freighter Madillion," she said, trying to salvage a little decorum.

"You guys in trouble?" the voice cut in.

"Since we are hanging here in space with smoke dribbling out of our engines, I suppose you could say that we were," she retorted.

"Well you better sort yourselves out, lady, cos you got company coming." The voice seemed to take savage delight in their plight.

"The scanner is out," snapped Raan. "We're blind." Hal stepped forward and took the link from Erion.

"Tranter, this is Hal. Can you get us out of here?"

"Hal old buddy! We meet in the strangest places. Are you having difficulties with our esteemed Galactic police?"

"You could say that," answered Hal dryly.

"There's another fighter squadron heading your way. Too many to take out, we'll have to run." He sounded miserable at the prospect of missing a fight. "I'll tow you; stand by for a tractor beam."

"Is he mad?" gasped Starfire, ignoring Hal's warning glare. "Tow the Madillion with that little thing?"

"Who said that?" demanded the voice. "Well whoever you are lady, you better strap yourself in cos I'm gonna show you what my baby can do."

"I hope you haven't upset him," hissed Hal. There was a jolt and Delta Ten said,

"That was a tractor beam. We are moving."

"He's towing us!" gasped Starfire. "I don't believe it."

"Believe it sweetheart," called Tranter. "Here we go."

"Light point one…two…three…" said Delta Ten.

"Better get strapped in, he's a maniac," snarled Hal, glaring at Starfire, who pulled a 'sorry' face.

"Light point eight….nine…" continued Delta Ten. There was a brief flash and the stars seemed to melt into a long blur. The crew on Madillion sat straight in their seats waiting for their ship to break up. "We have made the jump," stated the robot calmly. "We are now in hyperspace."

Starfire gazed at the controls worriedly. They might well have evaded capture by the galactic police but it would do them no good if the ship buckled under the strain. Metal creaked and groaned around them. She cast a look at the worried faces of Erion and Raan. "It'll hold out," she informed them. "Just for once, why can't we get from A to B without someone trying to blow us up?"

"We're alive," said Erion. "That's the main thing. Del, how about some coffee?"

"Hey Hal!" called Tranter. "I'd better take you to the base. You can tell me all your news and then we'll have a look at this lemon of yours, see what we can do with it."

"He has a base?" asked Starfire.

"The best equipped in the galaxy," admitted Hal.

"Then how come we've never heard of it?" asked Erion.

"Because you've never been on the wrong side of the law before." put in Raan.

"Something we'll have to get used to from now on," said Starfire sadly.

"We'll clear ourselves." declared Erion. "Have no fears on that score." She sounded quite definite but Raan and Starfire exchanged glances. They were not so sure.

"What have you done to upset our dear police force, Hal?" asked Tranter. "It isn't like you to go round attracting attention to yourself."

"It's a long story, Tran. How come you were so close to home?"

"Didn't you know?" began Tranter. "There's been a military coup. The Galactic Police have taken control of all Council Planets in the name of the Federation."

"What?" snapped four voices in unison.

"Where the hell have you guys been for the last forty eight hours?" muttered Tranter. "There was some sort of war between Terrell and Serrell. That's what I was doing hanging around there; you know, maybe pick up a few good wrecks to tow home. Well, in the meantime, some tin pot general called Roland used the diversion to take control. The guy must have been planning this for years, just waiting for the right moment."

"What about the Marines?" asked Erion.

"Search me; how should I know?" called Tranter. "As long as they leave me alone I couldn't give a hoot who's in charge. Well, we have another nine hours before we come out of this. I'm going to use the time to get some shut eye. See you one the other side." He cut the link.

"A coup," muttered Erion. "My father played right into their hands."

"I don't know Erion," put in Starfire. "I think we were just in the wrong place at the wrong time."

"Your father would have been killed anyway," said Hal flatly. "He would never have agreed to this."

"You're right," began Erion, "He was murdered, wasn't he?" There was no answer to this, and then Delta Ten entered with four cups of coffee on a tray.

"I have been checking out the rest of this vessel," he said, "There are facilities to cater for seven crew. Apart from the crew lounge there is a large cabin for the captain, and two smaller berths with three bunks each."

"You think we ought to keep this wreck?" asked Raan.

"If it was fixed up, it could be okay." answered Starfire, "It handles well for its size. We're not in the Marines now, Captain. How else are we going to get around?"

She's right, Raan," said Erion. "We need a ship and this one will have to do till we can trade it in for something smaller. "Starfire and I will share the captain's cabin. Del, can you ready it for us, and then fix up the other two for Hal and Raan?" ordered Erion.

"Of course, Major." He bowed stiffly and left.

"We might as well try and get some rest," she added, stretching and yawning. "We have nine hours to kill and we might as well make the best of it. Who's for first watch and who's for sleep? Raan, Hal?"

"He's way ahead of you," grinned Starfire. She motioned with her head at the gun man. He still sat at the gunnery post, his head resting on folded arms, leaning on his combat computer, asleep.

CHAPTER 13

"We're slowing," called Starfire from the pilot section. "We are in normal space."

"We're alive," said Erion, shaking her head.

"Where are we?" asked Starfire, thumping the navi-com. "This thing isn't working."

"We should be in the Keloran Sector," answered Hal.

"Never heard of it," she muttered, giving the navi-com one last, hopeful tap. She glanced at the rest of her instruments, most of which either glowed red, or were not working at all.

"That crazy nut has ruined my ship."

"Hey, Madillion, this is Tranter. Can you manoeuvre?"

"Just about," said Starfire, stiffly.

"I'm cutting you free, follow me." There was a small jolt and Madillion started to drift. Starfire used the ship's thrusters to propel it towards the mass of floating hulks that they neared. It was a ship's graveyard on a massive scale. They followed Tranter, who weaved slowly in and out between the wrecks until a large, battered looking station could be seen. It roughly resembled a sphere with docking arms and cranes jutting out from several points on it. "Dock at number three." He lit up an arm for them and Starfire headed for it, docking at the second attempt.

"Let's go meet this ship wrecker," she said, cutting the power and standing up.

"I think you'll be in for a surprise," said Hal quietly.

"After what we've been through I doubt anything would surprise me," said Erion. As she passed Hal, he caught her arm, making her wince. "He's my friend, Lady Erion." She stopped and looked up at him, perplexed. Her father was titled, and now he was dead, she inherited that title and the rights that went with it, but to give her credit, she had not given the matter any thought until now.

"I don't understand." she began.

"You will," he said softly. He looked at the others. "Any slight to him I'll take personally." He glared at them all in turn and pushed his way out of the section, leaving them all open mouthed.

"He's more of a robot than Delta Ten," muttered Raan as he followed the tall gun man down the corridor.

Tranter was there to greet them at the hatch. He was shorter than Hal and dressed in a dirty old space suit with illegal patches on it. Thick black hair framed a handsome, intelligent face, out of which twinkled two green eyes, flecked with copper. His skin was golden brown and immediately reflected his mixed parentage. Con Tranter was a Terrellian/Aurian half breed. Starfire stepped forward, appraising the man honestly and liking what she saw. He met her gaze without flinching and she held out her hand for him to take. He took her hand and shook it warmly, favouring her with a wicked grin. Starfire guessed that he had fought long and hard to get what he had, probably against more prejudice than she would ever have to face.

"You're a Terry!" he exclaimed to Starfire, looking her up and down. His face broke into a wide smile. "Welcome to my station." Raan came next and Tranter held up his palm, Aurian fashion. "The celebrated Captain Raan; I've heard of you. Is it true you're the greatest pan player this side of the galaxy?"

"Want to find out?" asked Raan with a grin, taking an immediate liking to the young man and surprised at himself for doing so. The joining of Terrellians with Aurians was socially unacceptable and frowned upon in the extreme, especially by the Terrellians, and any offspring, or 'Aurells' as they were called, were given a hard time of things as a result. Before meeting Hal and Starfire, Raan might have been less enthusiastic about Tranter. Now he shook him warmly by the hand, the strength of his grip taking Raan by surprise, for he looked slender underneath the bulky suit. Hal stepped forward, nodded quickly and didn't offer his hand. Tranter acknowledged the curt greeting, and turned to Erion, a broad grin creasing his features and making him look ten years younger.

"Hello," she said simply, holding out a slender hand in Terrellian fashion.

"Hi," he leered, turning to Hal. "Where did you find all these interesting people? It isn't like you to fraternise with the human race."

"It's a long story, Tran." answered the saturnine gunman. Delta Ten had remained aboard Madillion and Erion raised her wrist link to speak to him.

"Keep scanning Del, and let me know if anything comes too close." Tranter leaned towards her.

"There's no need for that, honey. This place is well hidden, and anyway, I have my own auto scanners out there."

"Did you get that, Del?" asked Erion. "It's safe to join us."

"Yes, Major," came back the answer. He emerged through the hatch to be greeted by Tranter, who studied him closely. Delta Ten lifted his palm and bowed his head in the Aurian fashion.

"Hi," said Tranter.

"How do you do, sir," answered Del. Tranter studied Delta Ten closely and made to walk away. He stopped and turned back, his hand raised as if he was about to ask a question, then he seemed to change his mind and shrugged.

"Hey, I'm forgetting my manners. Are you guys hungry?"

"I could eat a wanga." answered Erion.

"Come on then, Jemmi loves entertaining." He strode off down the corridor without looking back and Madillion's crew shuffled along behind like a school outing. Half the lights were out and pieces of spacecraft were everywhere. The odd dismantled robot blocked their path from time to time, and discarded computers were stacked floor to ceiling in odd corners, blocking the emergency hatchways. "Step into my office," said Tranter as they turned a corner and approached a large hatch. He pressed his palm against the indent for that purpose and the door slid open. He motioned the girls in first and they stepped forward to gaze appreciatively at the furnishings.

The room was massive, with one wall and half the ceiling made of a transparent material so that the outside star field was visible. This half of the room was taken up with a swimming pool and fountains, pale sand and ultra violet lights. Sun loungers dotted the poolside and on one of these, a long legged

Aurian beauty lay, completely naked and face down. At their entrance, she looked up and smiled, tossed her long chestnut hair over her shoulders and stood up without shame, to tie a robe around her body.

"Hal." she said warmly, walking up to him with a sensual grace and kissing him on the cheek. She stood back to appraise the others while Tranter introduced them. Her gaze lingered on Raan's face and he favoured her with a broad smile.

"Could you cook us up something while we talk, honey?" asked Tranter.

"Sure," she smiled, undulating over to the main computer stack in the centre of a sunken seating area. She punched out a sequence on the keyboard and then spoke to it. "Dinner for seven right away, Max. Bring it straight in."

"Yes Madam." answered a deep, metallic voice. She joined the others on a semi circular couch, curling up at Tranter is side like a huge cat.

"There is no need to bring food for me," began Delta Ten. "I do not eat."

"I knew it!" Tranter leapt out of his seat, pointing in triumph. "You're a humanified machine, a robot!"

"That is correct." Delta Ten bowed his head in salute.

"How did you guess?" asked Erion.

"I had an inkling something wasn't right when I met him. He looks real cute, but there's no warmth in the eyes. You get to learn a lot about judging folks when you're in the scrap spacer business. Then, when he didn't turn a hair when Jemmi stood up, I was reduced to two guesses." He looked at Del again, "You're good though. You'd fool most folks."

"He's an experimental model," explained Erion. "He has a positronic learning brain."

"Good for him!" muttered Tranter. "Now then, I want to know how you all ended up here." He rubbed his slender hands together with glee, "Tell me all about it." Slowly at first, starting at the beginning and missing out nothing, Erion told Tranter of the events that had led them to their present situation.

"Quite a tale." he said after she finished. "So you're the old man's little girl." he caught Hal's eye. "You going to take the Lady to Thirty Seven?"

"Yeah,"

"You'll need a ship. I can't let you have the Rebel, it's voice operated. You can take Jemmi's hopper; It'll get you there."

"Can you fix up the ship." asked Hal.

"That wreck of yours is pretty banged up, Hal It'll be pricey."

"It'll want the works, Tran."

"Then it'll be extortionate." Tranter had the good grace to look apologetic.

"Can you wait for the money?" asked Hal, "I have some owing that should just about cover it."

"I have some savings," added Starfire.

"I haven't." said Raan, peering down at his feet. He looked up suddenly, his eyes gleaming, "Hey! How about if I play you for it."

"Pan?" asked Tranter quickly. One game, winner takes all. I like it!"

"How about if I play you for it," said Erion shyly. She looked demurely up at Tranter, her amber eyes glowing warmly.

"You play pan?" asked Tranter.

"Why wouldn't I ?" she countered.

"Major…" began Raan, as if to deliver a warning.

"Shut it, Captain." snapped Erion. "I know what I'm doing."

"But, on Serrell…" he began.

"You were just lucky Captain, that's all." She smiled warmly, brimming with apparent confidence. "I can take him. I really can. Trust me." Raan looked at his boots and mumbled an intelligible reply. He had the attitude of someone who really knew his commanding officer was about to make a huge mistake but lacked the courage to challenge her authority.

"Okay, Lady, you got yourself a game," said Tranter. "If I win, you owe me a million credits. If you win, I fix up your ship for free." He looked a little uncomfortable, "Can you afford to pay up if you lose?"

"Oh, yes," she answered, sadly. "Our estate on Auria is easily worth a million credits and I shan't be able to go back there now." Her bottom lip trembled and she looked so pathetic that Raan had to look away.

"I thought you told me Erion won that game on Serrell," murmured Hal in Starfire's ear.

"She did, and by a mile." she whispered back. Someone was about to get shaken down and Starfire had to admit she'd never seen it done better

"Here's my hand on it, sir," said Erion. They touched palms, the bargain sealed. The hatch slid open and a hover trolley entered, carrying several covered meals. It stopped by the table, its many linked appendages lifting off the serving dishes and setting the table in front of them.

"This is our robo butler," explained Tranter. "Max, say hello."

"How do you do?" asked the trolley. It had a low, grating, metallic voice that droned on in a monotone all on one level and Starfire took an instant dislike to it.

"We're all fine," answered Tranter. "Have you brought wine?"

"I took the liberty of bringing the twenty-nine, Sir." said the trolley, politely.

"Perfect, Max. After we've eaten, the lady and I will be going to play a little Pan. Bring in the card table will you?"

"Certainly, Sir." They ate the meal with relish, washing it down with fine wine and finishing with cigars. Max returned carrying the card table on its back and placed it in front of them, arranging the seating and the cards with dexterity. It withdrew on its silent cushion of air and Erion and Tranter took seats facing each other. He passed her the cards to shuffle, which she did, seeming neither awkward nor professional. Tranter watched her carefully. The game of Pan was more of a game of bluff than chance and much depended on the players giving nothing of their feelings away. The first two hands were a testing ground, Erion winning one and Tranter the other. Raan watched with a wry grin. He was skilled at the game himself but had been soundly beaten due to the fact of underestimating the young woman. Somehow, he didn't think Tranter would make the same mistake and he settled himself down to watch the game.

Starfire did not play Pan. Terrellians as a rule did not take unnecessary risks, which included gambling of any sort. She knew the rules as a matter of course, but she soon grew bored and her gaze swept the room. Hal and Jemmi were engrossed in conversation and there was no sign of Delta Ten. They had all been given the freedom to treat the base as their own, so she motioned to Raan that she was going for a walk. He nodded, then turned his attention back to the game. As soon as Starfire stepped through the door, she called Delta Ten on her wrist link. He answered at once and met her at one of the air lock junctions.

"Did you check out Tranter?" she asked.

"As far as I can tell, Con Tranter is what he appears to be."

stated the robot. "I have been in direct communication with his computers. They confirm all he says. He is a space ship engineer and his order books are full for the eighteen months. He has already instructed his robots to ready the Madillion for repairs."

"Anything else you can tell me?" asked Starfire.

"There have been several messages to Auria from this station in the past few months. The transmissions were in code but the recipient of the messages was a High Commissioner of the Aurian Council."

"Damn it!" snapped Starfire, "I really liked the guy. I wonder what he's up to? Do you think he intends to turn us in?" she asked, forgetting for a moment that she conversed with a logical machine.

"I am unable to formulate a progressive conclusion at this time." stated Delta Ten as if such a thing would be sacrilegious.

"Make an educated guess then." urged Starfire,

"I cannot say on the given information," answered Del stiffly. Starfire gave up.

"Have it your own way, I'm going back to see how Erion is doing. Keep digging, see what you can find out. Oh, and don't tell anyone what you're up to till you've checked with me." Going by the troubled look on Tranter's face, he was not having things all his own way. Although a large pile of chips was by his right hand, Erion's pile was greater by far. Raan caught her eye and gave her a broad wink. Starfire crossed the room to the pool, settled herself on a lounger, gazed up into the starlit sky and listened to the stilted conversation that arose from the card table.

"I see your ten thousand, and raise twenty," That was Erion.

"Your twenty, and twenty more." Tranter sounded confident. Starfire allowed herself to drift, then smiled and turned towards Raan as he touched her arm and drew up a chair to lie beside her.

"This is some place." he said, raising a hand to the sky. We could almost be outside."

"Yeah," agreed Starfire. Something in her voice made Raan look sideways at her.

"Still get the jitters outside?" Raan was referring to her Terrellian agoraphobic roots.

"No, not really," she answered. "I just don't see what all this fuss about the great outdoors is about."

"That's because you have no romance in your soul." He motioned to the sky with his cigar. "Nothing could be more romantic than a star lit night, a sandy beach, a beautiful girl and a...argh!" Starfire pushed him off his lounger and he rolled to his feet with the grace of a dancer. "As I said Lieutenant, you have no romance in your soul."

"What do you think of Tranter?" Starfire changed the subject.

"I like him. I don't exactly trust him, but he'd make a good Marine."

"Yeah, that's about what I thought too."

"Star, are you all right?" Raan turned over and lay on his front and closed his eyes. "You need a rest kid, that's your trouble. You worry too much." A yell rent the air and Raan gave a visible start, rolled off his lounger again and stood up with Starfire by his side, gun in hand. It was Erion, screaming for joy.

"I did it! I won!" Their thoughts forgotten, Raan and Starfire rushed towards the gleeful young woman. Raan reached her first and picked her up, planting huge kiss on her lips.

"You're all sandy!" she chastised. He placed her gently on the ground and they both stepped away from each other, clearly embarrassed at the spontaneous contact. Hal rushed forward, gun drawn and ready as Raan yelled in delight,

"Hey, Hal we gotta ship."

"Hooray for our side," he muttered darkly, sliding the big gun back into its holster.

"He's another one who should lighten up." mused Raan. "Maybe it's a 'Terry' thing?"

"If anything, I should be the one to worry," said Tranter. He took Erion's hand. "I have never been beaten by a more worthy or beautiful opponent." He led her to the couch. "Where the hell did you learn to play like that?" Erion smiled and looked down,

"Oh, you know, here and there. I stayed a while on Cariss. There isn't much more to do there than play Pan."

"Cariss," mused Tranter, "Now there's a jolly place. We may have a mutual friend." He visibly made an effort to smile. "A drink before we retire? Max!"

"Here sir," answered the hover trolley. It cracked open a new bottle with a metal claw and filled half a dozen glasses that were sitting on it's back.

"And what do you say, tin man?" Tranter clearly addressed Delta Ten but it was Starfire who spoke.

"He means you, Del."

"It seems a fair deal, Lieutenant," Delta Ten addressed Starfire. "The average price for a ship refit of this magnitude would be well under a million credits. Unless Mr Tranter is dishonest or incompetent we will not have to find further payment."

"That satisfy you?" Tranter deliberately ignored the slant on his character.

"It does," answered Erion. "Mr Tranter, we have a deal." They touched palms on it and took a drink.

"Tran, I'd like to take Erion over to see Thirty Seven tomorrow." said Hal.

"Sure, Hal. Do you know why you're going?" Hal shrugged.

"All I know is the old man asked me to take his precious over there." He turned his grey eyes towards Delta Ten, "You know anything else?"

"No Mr Hal. That is all the General said." Hal lifted his eyes in Erion's direction.

"That all right with you?"

"Of course it is." she answered. "Just what is this place? I have never heard of it."

"You wouldn't have, My Lady," said Tranter softly. Starfire risked a quick glance across at Raan. He was risking a quick glance across at her and their eyes met knowingly. It was obvious to them at least, that Erion and Tranter were fast becoming more than acquaintances.

"It's an outlaw haunt." said Hal. "Where murderers and thieves go to spend their money." He was unnecessarily blunt.

"Wait a minute," began Raan with rising excitement, "The Cantina. You mean the Cantina!"

"That's what you'd know it as," admitted Hal.

"The Marines and the Police have been trying to find that place for years," said Erion. "How did my father know about it?"

"He didn't know where it was," began Hal, "But he knew how to get a message there. He rated a lot of respect or he wouldn't have been trusted."

"You all keep saying you know my father," blurted Erion. "He would never consort with criminals…" she tailed off, looking at Hal who gave a wry smile.

"Lady, you have a lot to learn."

"Believe me Hal, I don't intend to stay on this side of the fence for very long, I can tell you." said Erion, stiffly. Hal and Tranter exchanged looks.

"You're naïve," stated Hal. He was stopped by a warning head shake from Tranter. The lithe engineer took her hand in his own."

"Erion," he began, looking deep into her eyes. "Like Hal says, you have a lot to learn about the big world out there." He took her empty glass from her hand and placed it back on the hover trolley. "Come here and sit down." He gently pushed her unresisting form onto the couch. "It isn't you; the fault lies with the Marines. They take you when you're kids and bring you up in a way that separates you from the rest of the galaxy. Maybe Raan knows a little of what goes on, but there's corruption, extortion, murder, bribery. All of this has been acceptable in the Marines and the Police for years, and it's been getting worse. Your father knew this, and he was killed because he tried to do something about it. Nooran was a good man too and his death has spelled the end of everything good about the administration. Don't you see, the corruption goes right to the top now. I know you love the Marines but we must be able to trust you. I know it'll go against everything you believe in, but we need your solemn oath." Erion looked confused and Tranter turned to the others in exasperation. "Can't any of you get through to her."

"I think what Tranter is trying to say," began Starfire, "Is that whatever you think personally, you must give your word not to betray the whereabouts of this 'Cantina' to the authorities."

"I see," said Erion. "Why didn't he say that then?"

"I did," began Tranter, "Didn't I?"

"Very well," Erion came to a decision. "Since it is obvious that you will not take me unless you have it, my word is given that I will not betray the whereabouts of your criminal outpost."

"A Marine's word is good enough for me." said Tranter. He looked up, "Hal?"

"We'll leave first thing tomorrow."

"While you're gone, I'll make a start on your ship. He looked at Raan and Starfire. You guys can give me a hand."

"Sure," answered Raan. He stood up. "I'm going to turn in." He drained his champagne glass, placed it on the trolley and the others followed suit. In their quarters, Starfire and Erion lay on their bunks looking up at the ceiling.

"What a week!" sighed Starfire.

"You said it, Lieutenant." They lay in silence with their own thoughts for a moment, then Erion turned on her side to face Starfire.

"What do you think of Tranter?" she asked.

"I don't know, Major. He's a little crazy. Do you know he told me he flipped a coin to decide whether to save us or not. Starfire took a deep breath. "I wouldn't get too close to him you. We hardly know the guy."

"I trust him." smiled Erion. Her face hardened. "Starfire, so much has happened to me in the last few days, I can't believe it. The Marines was my life."

"Mine too," admitted Starfire. "I never thought someone like me could fit into this crazy galaxy any other way, but I've met Hal and Tranter and they seem to get along okay in it. Tranter's right; we have a hell of a lot to learn." Erion nodded.

"I think I'm going to learn a lot more tomorrow." She yawned and said, "Computer, lights down to ten percent!." The lighting dimmed and they turned over in their bunks and went to sleep.

CHAPTER 14

"All set?" asked Hal, as he and Erion sat in Jemmi's little planet hopper.

"I'm ready," she answered.

"Disengage," ordered Hal. The small ship broke free from the station arm and drifted slowly away. Hal fired the thrusters and the ship weaved in and out of the floating hulks with ease.

"You never told us you could pilot a ship," said Erion in a slightly accusing tone.

"You never asked," grunted Hal.

"This is going to be a really fun trip," she muttered under her breath.

"Sarcasm from you Major. Whatever is the galaxy coming to?"

"What's our heading?" she asked, refusing to be drawn into verbal banter. Hal leant over her and punched the course into the computer. "No hyperspace," she remarked. "It's in this sector then?"

"You'll know soon enough," began Hal, "But if we wanted, we could be there and back less than two days."

"Oh," answered Erion softly. She lifted her head slightly to gaze across at the readout from the little navi-com screen in front of Hal. They seemed to be headed for a very large asteroid field and their course was plotted straight through the middle of it. She turned in her seat to face him.

"You can't mean to fly straight into that?"

"Why not?" he countered. "That's where we're going." He grinned as the realisation dawned. "That's the Marine's weakness," he stated. Erion was pleased to note that he did not seem to lump her in with them now. Everything has always been worked out for them, from the Academy right up to their pensioning off. They've never been desperate enough to want to hide in an asteroid field so they never thought of looking there." Hal chose his words with care. "Marines are the armies; the tactical arm of the Federation. They fight wars, bring back trophies and call it peacekeeping. If a planet can't defend itself against attack, that's tough luck on them. The Galactic Police, now they're another story."

"We're not overly fond of them ourselves you know," answered Erion. "They seemed a good idea at the start of the Federation, when we needed order on a galactic scale, but things have become out of control. They have too much power now."

"They control more than you think," stated Hal flatly. He busied himself with piloting the little ship and Erion soon became bored watching the unchanging star map and fidgeted in her seat. The hopper had no sleeping quarters but the twin seats at the front were designed for great comfort. Erion tilted the seat back, stretched out as much as she could in the padded co pilot's couch and turned her head sideways to watch the tall

Terrellian as he piloted the hopper with ease. His hair, she noticed, was fair and it curled very slightly at the ends. Aurians had strong hair that never lost its chestnut colour and his looked unusually pale and wispy. Now she was getting used to it, his skin didn't look as sickly and pale. It had a slight brown tinge to it that was probably due to some sort of ultra violet exposure. It was his eyes that fascinated her though. They were dull, grey, expressionless eyes that gave nothing away of the thoughts that must lie beneath. The only time they showed any emotion was when he had killed Dolton Blass. Then they had glinted like polished steel...

"Cantina Control, this is Planet Hopper Jemmi One. Come in please." Erion jerked upright at the sudden words. Her neck ached and she realised she had been asleep. She stretched in the co pilot's seat and rubbed her shoulder, rolling her head around to ease the nagging cramp that had developed. Hal was easing the craft towards a panorama of massive rocks that seem to stretch for infinity on front of them. A glance at her wrist link showed Erion that over four hours had passed but the gunman looked calm and refreshed.

"This is Cantina Control, Jemmi One." The man's voice sounded calm and competent. "What is your status, over?"

"Requesting assisted passage through the field. Over?"

"Please transmit your recognition code and disengage your navi-computer." Hal did so and slowed the ship as they approached the outer edge of the asteroids. Huge revolving boulders and many smaller rocks blocked their way as far as the eye could see but there seemed to be many paths that they could take. Erion wisely kept silent and waited until one of the larger rocks left the throng and floated towards them. It halted in front of them and emitted a pulsing green light every five seconds or so. "We confirm your navi-com is off line. Do you see your guide, Jemmi One?" asked the flight controller.

"Right on cue, Cantina. We'll see you soon. Over and out." The boulder backed away from them and entered the revolving rocks. The pulsing light was easy to spot and Hal guided the little ship into the maze behind it. There were many twists and turns and Erion guessed the route was deliberately elaborate. Their path had been cleared of smaller missiles and was wide enough to take a freighter with care but it would have been virtually impossible to find a way through without a guide or programmed co-ordinates. Erion stared out of the port, lost in her own thoughts. She had no idea what was waiting for her at this Cantina, but what was more frightening was the truth of Hal's words. Her life was no longer ordered. Erion was a career soldier. She went where she was told to go and carried out her orders when she got there. Life took care of itself. Erion was proud of her Marine career. She was Highborn and could have done anything she wanted and had chosen to be in the Marines like her father. Now Hal's words caused her to think again. Of course there was corruption and violence among certain quarters; her stint as Erion the dancer on the mining colonies had taught her that much. The Marines and the police did as good a job of maintaining order as anyone could, she was sure of that; or she had been sure until five days ago.

"Do you think I should have changed out of uniform?" she asked him. "I'll stick out like a wanga on a snow drift." He shot her a withering glance that left her feeling incredibly naïve. She was used to being in command and didn't like the sensation. To hide her confusion, she made a great pretence of peering downward at the small haphazard patch of uninteresting buildings that came into view as Hal steered to hopper to a small planetoid. He went down slowly, placed the craft with great care on an ancient creaking pad and cut the engines with a grateful sigh. It was the only sign he gave that the trip had been any strain on him and it passed as soon as it came. Erion realised that she was beginning to read him better. As a Marine, she could handle any potentially dangerous situation that came her way. She could navigate a class Ten Battle Cruiser across the galaxy and she could command a crack troop of soldiers with confidence but she didn't know people. Ordinary people baffled her and she suddenly realised that she despised them for their normality. At first, she had intensely disliked Hal. She thought it was revulsion at his chosen profession but she was beginning to realise that it was a little racial prejudice mixed with a lot of jealousy. Somehow, Hal had known a part of her father that she had never been allowed to see.

The ship started to drop below the surface of the little planet, accompanied by the creaks and groans of well worn machinery clanking into motion. They made a jerky descent for thirty seconds and stopped with a slight jolt. Hal was waiting by the hatchway and opened it as soon as the green light showed the chamber was pressurised. Erion stepped out behind him and followed him to some aircar doors, noting on the way the various ships that sat in the large silo. The aircar was old but well maintained. It sped along and slightly downwards for less than a minute before it stopped and opened its doors upon a scene that Erion would always remember with pleasure.

The room was discreetly but tastefully lit, with just the slightest tinge of blue. There was a faint scent of fruity cigar smoke overlaid with gently perfumed air and the plaintive strains of Valasian jazz filtered through the sounds of people enjoying a meal at the many scattered tables. The room was circular, the centre taken up by a raised dais upon which was displayed an abstract holographic image that was linked by computer to the music. It gave a pleasing picture to the eye but it did not dominate the senses. It could have been a high class club in any corner of the galaxy, mused Erion, as she strolled behind Hal to the bar that ran half the length of the circular wall in front of them. She could see now why he had scorned the suggestion of her changing out of uniform, for at least three separate groups of Marines were seated at tables, either drinking or playing pan.

"Hal!" said the plump little waitress behind the bar. "Long time no see."

"Thirty Seven in?" Hal wasted no time in idle chatter, but the girl's smile stayed across her features as if glued there.

"He's running a big Pan game in the back," she answered, nodding to a red light that glowed above the bar.

"Tell him I'm here with a Lady." Hal placed special emphasis on the last word, which caused the waitress to take a curious look at Erion.

"I'll go tell him," she muttered, turning away.

"Hey, you!" Hal glanced up towards the bar mirror to see three unshaven Aurians walking towards them. The rest of the customers sidled away from the bar to watch as the three men stopped, forming a rough semi circle in front of Hal.

"You came in Tranter's Planet Hopper." The middle one snarled, watching Hal's face carefully. The man on his left scanned the room in the reflection of the bar mirror, while the other fixed Erion with a leer.

"Well spotted," said Hal softly, turning to face them. "Now if that's all you wanted to say...."

"You're Hal aren't you?" the first man cut in. He wiped a

grimy hand across his mouth. "There's a big fifty on your head, mister."

"Hey," called a grizzled old man from further along the bar. "There's a rule here about bounties. Nobody tries for 'em and if anybody dies here, the house collects."

"Stay outa this!" snapped the leader of the trio. He lurched and belched loudly, the fetid smell of his drunken breath reaching Erion. She tensed by Hal's side, her hand hanging loosely by the flap of her holster. She wasn't practised in the art of the fast draw but she was trained to Marine standards in the use of her pistol. With a little luck she might take one of them out."

"It's okay, Orlando." Hal answered the old man but didn't take his eyes of the three scruffy Aurians in front of him. "Erion, get out of the way." When had turned to face the men, Hal had leaned on the bar with his elbows. Now he straightened and repeated his words to her without looking away from the men.

"Yeah, do like he says, Erion!" sneered the smallest man. He wore the uniform of a Marine private but it was heavily soiled and Erion pegged him as her mark. She hated deserters but she moved a few paces away from Hal and waited for the fun to start.

"You figure to try for the bounty on my head, mister?" Hal's voice was hardly more than a whisper and Erion prepared to make her move. She knew from experience that when Hal spoke softly, he was making ready for the kill.

"There's three of us to your one, Hal. I don't care how good you are, you can't get all of us before one of us downs you. Hal didn't answer but just stood facing the three men, his hands hanging loosely by his side. The small man began to sweat more heavily and did not look as sure of himself.

"We gonna take him, Stace?"

"Naw..." answered the leader, turning away. "He's too good for us, Joey." He suddenly spun around to face Hal, his gun drawn and ready. It was a well practiced move and had worked before but this time the three were facing someone who was just as devious as they were. Hal shot the leader through the heart, the laser bolt ripping a hole the size of a man's fist in his chest. The charge dissipated quickly as the gun was set for killing close up. The other two were not as fast as their leader and Hal had time to pick his shots with care. Both men fell with wounds to their legs, their guns still half drawn. All this had taken just over a second and Erion was still lifting her Marine issue pistol from its holster. Like most of the other people in the room, she was stunned into inability at the speed of the cold eyed gunman's shooting.

"Don't kill us, mister," whined the small man lying in a pool of blood on the plush red carpet. His leg had been blown off at the knee. The shock of the wound was beginning to wear off and the pain was setting in. The wounded man looked down at the ghastly horror of his leg and screamed, 'My leg! I've lost my leg!" Hal looked dispassionately down and hooked his toe under the scorched limb lying nearby. He nudged it over to the stricken man.

"No you haven't. Here it is." He grabbed Erion by the arm and pulled her away, still staring down at the carnage on the cantina floor. A door opened at the side of the bar, and a tall, battered, black robot with glowing amber eyes stood just outside it. He bowed as they reached him.

"Hal! I expected you sooner." He spoke in a warm baritone which was completely at odds with his metallic appearance.

"We had a little trouble Thirty Seven."

"So I see. I was hoping someone would tend to those three deserters. Your handiwork has netted us seven thousand credits in bounty money." He lifted a black hand to Erion, who touched its palm with her own. "Welcome to my establishment. You must be Dorian's daughter. You favour him, my dear. Come into my office and I will give you what he left in my keeping." As the seven foot robot turned and walked out of the bar, Erion could see he was limping. They followed him into a semi circular room and the creaking robot eased himself behind a large mahogany desk, situated near to the curved wall. He leaned slightly forward and motioned for them to sit in one of the four arm chairs that were placed facing the desk. When they were seated, he offered them both refreshments, which they declined. Realising that Erion wished to get down to business straight away, he placed his elbows on the desk and made a steeple of his fingers. "The General sent word here to me six months ago that something big was in the wind. He warned me to be extra careful whom I trusted and sent a package for me look after. If he was to die an unnatural death, I was to wait another three months for you to claim the package. If you had not done so in that time I was to open it myself." Thirty Seven leaned sideways and opened a drawer in his desk and pulled out a small plastic box, handing it to Erion. Will you be staying long with us?" he asked.

"Just tonight," answered Hal.

"Tell Orlando to give you our best suite on the house," said the robot. He put his large black head on one side in a strangely human looking gesture and said to Erion, "I am sorry about your father, my dear, he was a trusted friend."

"It seems that there is much to learn about my father," began Erion. Hal took her arm.

"Come on Major," he said softly, leading her out. There was no sign of the fight in the bar room and Hal steered Erion further along the bar to the old man who had called out the warning about bounties. He was wearing a battered old flying jacket and stood taking glasses out of the automat.

"Orlando," nodded Hal.

"How are you, son?" asked the old man. He grinned at Erion, showing a row of broken teeth. "Does my old eyes good to see the boy in action. There's nobody can beat him."

"There's always somebody faster," answered Hal, waving aside a request for a drink. "Thirty Seven said to give us the VIP suite."

"Sure, boy," He handed Hal a thin computer cardkey. "You know the way." Hal took the key and they walked over to the aircar. They didn't have to wait and it soon deposited them in a long corridor, flanked with doors. Hal walked to the farthest one and inserted the computer key in the slot. The door slid open and they walked inside. It was furnished in pale blue and gold and comprised of a double bedroom, a sitting room and a bathroom. Erion plonked herself down on the couch and accepted a drink from Hal, who sat beside her on a comfy chair and waited while she opened her package. It comprised of a computer data card and a recording crystal. The latter showed full, so Erion inserted it into the slot of a console built into the arm of the settee. The screen on the wall lit up to show her father's kind face. He was in uniform and standing in front of the huge false fireplace in their manor house on Auria. He was clearly relaxed and held a drink in one hand and a half smoked cigar in the other.

"My darling daughter," he began, "I sincerely hope that it is you who is watching me now. You have just left for the mining colonies, and in a way, I hope you will never see this, for if you do, it will mean that I am dead and my death is no accident. You must be strong, Erion and you must never lose faith in the Marines and what they stand for." He took a sip from his brandy glass and continued. "For many years now, there has been a subversive element filtering into the Aurian Marines. The Admiral, myself and several other high ranking officers have tried and failed to find out the names of any instigators, but we do know that they are also highly ranked and powerful. Now that I am dead, it will probably mean that there has begun a movement to take complete control of the Aurian Federation and the Marines. You must fight them, Erion and stop them any way you can. Thirty Seven should have given you everything you will need in your task. I have placed the code to unlock the information inside the memory circuits of the android, Delta Ten. He will give up this information on hearing the trigger words 'Eleanor Carrie'. Contact Admiral Nooran. He will help you and there are other names mentioned in this crystal. Trust no one else unless you are absolutely sure of their integrity. There isn't much more for me to say, darling, but Goodbye and Good Luck. Try to live well and die with honour. I love you, my dear, never forget that." The screen darkened and Erion sat in front of it in silence for long minutes. She was dimly aware that Hal was speaking to her and made a mental effort to jerk herself back to the present.

"Do you want to go straight back to the base?" he asked.

"No, Hal. You can't fly all that way on manual without rest. Go on, I'll be all right." The gunman nodded and walked to the bathroom to freshen up before getting some much needed sleep. Erion watched him go, then pushed back the little disk to watch the recording again.

CHAPTER 15

Starfire and Raan watched Jemmi's hopper wend its way though the derelict hulks carrying Hal and Erion on their way to the Cantina. Tranter walked silently up to them and clapped them both on the shoulder.

"Time enough for star gazing later, we got work to do." He gave Starfire a friendly shove to get her going and the three of them walked off down the corridor.

'Sir," Delta Ten said from a side hatchway, "I have located the twin engine bomber you requested and I have instructed your robot cranes to bring it into the bay."

"Good, I'll come with you now and take a look at it, see if we can cut the engines free."

"How long will this refit take, Tranter?" asked Raan, "It's not that I want to hurry you or anything, but half the galaxy is out there looking for us and I don't like the thought of us being here without a ship to fight from." Tranter thumped his arm.

"Don't worry pal, you're safe here with me. The galactic

police have been looking for this place for years and have never found it. Anyway, it's well protected and screened against their scanners. And to answer your question, it should take about three months to…"

"Three months!" blurted Starfire.

"Come on kid, what did you expect?" shouted Tranter. "You want a complete refit, don't you? That means new engines, new linkages, new computer systems, new hydraulics. The old stuff has to be taken out, and the new stuff put in and linked up. How long did you think it was gonna take?" Starfire shook her head.

"You're right of course, I should have realised." She looked at Raan. "But three months…"

"Look," began Tranter, "I have a ship for sale that might suit you. It's a class eight Corvette, modified to haul specials."

"Specials?" asked Starfire.

"Contraband." supplied Raan. Tranter had the good grace to look sheepish.

"Yeah, well the engines will do light six and the modified bomb bay means you can haul a fair piece of freight. She's smaller than a standard but that means she's faster and more manoeuvrable. There's an upgraded defence system and two extra guns over and above standard. I could take your old wreck in part exchange. What do you say? At least have a look at her."

"How much do you want for her?" asked Raan, getting right to the point.

"Four; but for you, and with Madillion thrown in, two fifty."

"Two and a half million?" asked Starfire aghast," You must be joking!"

"What about the million you owe us?" asked Raan.

"That'll take it down to one and a half million creds. What do you say?"

"We couldn't even scrape together one and half thousand," said Starfire miserably.

"You won't have to give it to me all in one go," explained Tranter. "Thirty Seven and I have a deal going. He will lend you the money to buy the ship and you can pay him back in instalments."

"With a little interest thrown in of course," added Raan.

"We all have to make a living, pal."

"We'll have to talk it over with Erion and Hal when they get back," sighed Starfire. Tranter caught her eye and made as if to speak, then stopped.

"What is it?" she asked.

"Well, I wouldn't include Hal in any of your future plans, I don't think he figures to stick around."

"Has he said anything to you about leaving?" asked Starfire.

"He doesn't tell anyone what he's doing but I know he prefers to work alone. From what Erion has told me, he signed up with you for a job favour owed to the General. Now his job's been done, I figure he'll take off once he's brought your Major back."

"You could be right at that," began Raan. "But we'll wait and see. He needs a personality transplant, but he's good in a fight and we'll need him."

"You do have a way with words, Raan," smiled Starfire.

"What do you say we have the rest of the day off." suggested Tranter. "I'll hold off making any changes to your ship until the others get back. Hal figured on two days at the most."

"That should give me plenty of time to get a good tan on this wonderful body." sighed Raan. He grinned at Jemmi, who had just turned the corner, and grabbed her elbow, spun her around and led her away without breaking her stride. His voice could be heard fading away along the metal corridors. "Has anyone ever told you of the benefits of lounging by a pool and soaking up those good old ultra violet rays?" The two watched them go and Starfire smiled at Tranter.

"She is very beautiful. Don't you ever get jealous?" Tranter actually looked surprised at the question, then he smiled.

"Listen, a lot of folks get the wrong idea about Jemmi and me. We stay together because that's the way we like it. Jem can leave any time she likes. She's a free agent and so am I."

"I noticed," muttered Starfire under her breath. Tranter chose not to hear and steered the conversation towards flying, a subject close to both their hearts. They were still discussing the pros and cons of the magnetic jet propulsion system when they reached the lounge. Raan was already face down on a lounger at the edge of the pool while Jemmi applied liberal amounts of tanning gel to his naked back.

"How does he do it?" asked Starfire. "If we landed on a mining colony he would find a harem." She threw some cold water over his back, smiled warmly at the sound of his muted scream and leaned over to whisper in his ear, "I thought you might like to see our new ship," began Starfire, "but it's patently obvious you have much more important things to do."

"I have every faith in you, Lieutenant," he said with a yawn, settling back into his cushions. "I'll expect a full report over dinner." Later that evening, the four sat around the table, delighting in a meal that would put a top Aurian restaurant to shame. The conversation and the wine flowed freely, and it was late that night, by Aurian Standard Time, that they retired to their rooms.

Not too far away, deep inside a barren asteroid, Erion finally succumbed to sleep. Hal slid from the bed and walked into the study. He switched off the vid screen and covered her with a blanket. Only then did he return the bed and relax into a dreamless sleep himself.

Hal set himself five hours to rest, and he was not surprised to awaken only ten minutes before this time. He bathed, removed his clothes from the auto valet, dressed and buckled on his gun belt before he walked into the sitting room. Erion was also awake, but she was sitting up on the couch, her knees tucked under chin and the blanket draped around her shoulders, sipping hot coffee. Hal poured himself one from the food machine and sat opposite her in the easy chair.

"If it's okay by you, we'll have breakfast, then I'll take you back." He lit a thin black cigar and permitted himself a sigh of pleasure as the acrid smoke slid into his lungs. Erion noticed that he did almost everything with his left hand, unconsciously leaving his gun hand free.

"Don't you ever relax?" she asked him, He shook his head briefly.

"Too many enemies."

"But you can't live on your nerves all the time."

"I'm used to it."

"But surely..." He silenced her with a glare and stood up, walking to the door.

"Get dressed. I'll be in the bar."

"And thank you too!" muttered Erion under her breath as the tall gunman stalked out. She deliberately took her time, choosing to soak in the marble effect bath, floating amongst soap suds in hot scented water. She felt much better as she dressed, her mood dipping only slightly as she picked up her father's message and slipped the little crystal into her pocket. She had done her crying for him, now she must look forward.

She gave the room a quick look to make sure they had left nothing behind and went to join Hal in the bar.

Although it was early morning by Aurian Standard Time, there were people propping up the bar and drinking. She spotted Hal at a small table, sitting with his back to the wall and drinking coffee. She walked across the dance floor, sat next to him and ordered breakfast from the small com-link built into the table. Several interested glances were thrown their way and after a drone had delivered her breakfast and Erion had eaten it, two men and a woman walked up to the table and nodded to Hal. The tallest of the three, a handsome, rangy looking Aurian, threw Erion a lopsided grin and spoke in an offworlder drawl.

"Hal, mind if we meet your friend?"

"Be my guest," answered Erion." The three drew up chairs and sat down, the tall Aurian turning his chair around and sitting astride it.

"Hal, will you introduce us to the lady?"

"Sure," he murmured. "Erion, meet Jeddoh Cloud."

"How do you do?" Erion held out her palm and made sure she showed no surprise. Jed Cloud and his brothers were pirates and the Galactic Police had been on their trail for years. There was a substantial reward out for their capture, particularly for Jed, the oldest of the four. He certainly did not look like the sadistic killer and rapist he was suppose to be, but Erion reserved her judgement until she could talk to Hal.

"This is Elkrist," Jed motioned to the silver haired woman on his right. She was dark skinned and muscular, her glistening body adorned with metal armour and silver jewellery. Erion recognised her name. Elkrist was an infamous outlaw from the planet Valasia, trading on the lusts and greed of men all over the galaxy. Erion had to admit that she came well equipped to accomplish her aims and many a high ranking official had cause to rue the day he met the voluptuous princess. When she spoke, her voice was deep and vibrant, with only a slight trace of Valasian accent.

"I am pleased to make your acquaintance, I knew your father very well. Also, I think, we have a mutual acquaintance in Commander Jellon on mining colony Epsoid Seven, yes?" She turned up the corners of her mouth slightly in a grim parody of a smile. Erion could hardly repress a shudder as the memory of the man forced itself to the front of her mind. Elkrist continued, "I am sure he will be sadly missed."

"Missed?" asked Erion before she could stop herself. Jellon had been the chief of one of the mines on Cariss, where Erion had worked undercover as a dancer. He had been particularly obnoxious and news of any misfortune that had befallen him was welcome.

"He died," drawled Elkrist, "A most terrible accident. He fell into a rock crusher."

"Oh the poor man," sighed Erion. "Did he suffer, do you think?"

"Undoubtedly," answered Elkrist.

"Shame," said Erion, dryly. She began to warm to the other woman, deciding to trust her own judgement, rather than believe the wanted flyers put out by the Galactic Police. She turned to the third person, seeing a small insignificant Aurian man in his early thirties. He stood up to touch her palm and bowed politely.

"My name is Gant, My Lady. You won't have heard of me, but I intend to overthrow the Federation and I hope you and your friends will join us." Erion stared at him open mouthed for a moment then gathered her wits.

"I'll have to think about that, My Lord and I can't speak for my crew." Just in time, Erion noticed the ring that he wore on his little finger. It was the crest of one of the houses of Auria and proclaimed him to be a High Born like herself, probably of royal blood. Not to accord him the proper respect would have been unforgivable to her. He smiled with genuine warmth at her tactfulness.

"Please call me Gant. My home is nothing but a planet sized garrison for the Galactic Authorities now, as is Elkrist's. We have no Kingdoms to rule and no People to serve. There are no High Borns in the Alliance."

"Nor Low Borns neither," put in Jeddoh Cloud.

"Except Terrellians." smiled Elkrist, giving Hal a knowing look. Hal gave a lofty sniff and muttered something about the morals of Offworlders, and Erion suddenly realised she was in the privileged company of those people whom Hal called friends.

"I have not heard of this Alliance," said Erion.

"You would not have, My Lady," countered Gant.

"Please, call me Erion."

"Very well, Erion. You are a Major in the Space Marines. You would have been told only what the Federation wanted you to know. By the look on your face when we were introduced, I'd say you believed yourself to be in the company of the worst criminals in the history of the universe."

"You're right about that," she agreed, slowly realising the inner strength of the man. "I can only speak for myself, Gant, but I will put your request to the others when we return."

"That might not be possible for the moment," broke in Thirty Seven's voice from behind her. She turned in her seat to look up at the black machine.

"Why? What's wrong?" she asked.

"A routine scan of your ship has unearthed a tracing beacon. It is set on a Galactic Police frequency and was transmitting. Luckily the asteroid belt has strong magnetic fields which would have prevented any signal reaching its intended destination."

"But I don't know anything about it," gasped Erion, looking wildly at the disbelieving faces around her. "Hal, tell them please." She stared hopefully into his grey eyes, searching in vain for a sign of warmth.

"Well we know damn well it wasn't Hal," snarled Jeddoh cloud, his hand on his gun.

"Could it have been one of your crew?" asked Elkrist.

"Never," snapped Erion.

"You have only known them for five days. Are you willing to stake your life on that?" asked Gant gently.

"Yes," answered Erion without hesitation. Hal stood up.

"We have to get back to the station."

"Very well," said Gant. The others stood up to let Hal past and Erion made to follow him but Jeddoh Cloud grabbed her arm.

"Hal figures you're okay lady, and that's fine by me. But if I find out you're lying…"

"I'll kill her myself," put in Hal, who had returned when he saw Erion wasn't behind him. Jed released her, smiling once again. "Hey, remember us to Tran, will you?"

"Sure," began Hal, catching Gant's eye. "I'll find out where the bug came from," he promised. Once inside the aircar, Erion permitted herself a long sigh.

"I think I just met some very special people."

"You did," agreed Hal. "They will do what they said."

"You mean overthrow the Federation?"

"Not them perhaps, but they've started the ball rolling and others have joined."

"Do you belong to this Alliance?" she asked.

"No," he answered. The aircar doors opened out onto the spacer park and Hal strode forward. Erion scuttled after him, almost running to keep up.

"If the others agree when I ask them, would you come in with us?"

"No," answered Hal. He gave the firm impression that it would do no good to press him further on the matter. They reached the little planet hopper, climbed in and strapped themselves into the couches. Hal lifted off straight away, wanting to get back to Tranter's base as soon as he could.

"You have an idea who planted that bug, don't you?" stated Erion. Hal looked sharply at her, not liking the idea of someone reading his thoughts so well. He didn't answer her, but heaved back on the controls sharply and the ship lurched to one side, pulling away from the asteroid at a sharp angle. Erion looked down to hide her smile then stretched out to gain as much comfort as she could for the journey back.

CHAPTER 16

Starfire sighed and switched off the monitor she had been reading. She looked at the time on her wrist link and called over to Delta Ten, who was welding a small linkage at a nearby bench.

"How long till the hopper docks, Del?"

"Eighteen minutes and forty two seconds," answered Delta Ten, not looking up from his task. It had not taken long for boredom to set in on Tranter's base, and Starfire had eagerly agreed to help the young man with his work. Raan was off somewhere by the pool and had hardly moved from there at all in the last thirty hours.

"Better give Raan a buzz and let him know," suggested Starfire. "I suppose he'll want to be here when they get in." Raan joined them fifteen minutes later and they watched the little ship come into view and weave it's way between the resting derelict ships to dock. The inner hatch opened to reveal Erion, smiling warmly. Hal was two paces behind her, his expression blank as usual.

"You see Hal," she smiled, looking at the dishevelled Starfire and Delta Ten. "As soon as I'm not around, discipline goes straight out of the window."

"We have been working," said Starfire, throwing the by now golden skinned Raan a dark look. "Not like some I could mention." Raan looked injured.

"Some people eat work, Star, and some of us are more delicate. After a strenuous mission, it says in the manual that rest and recreation is most important."

"R and R maybe." began Starfire, "not total inertia."

"Where's Tran?" snapped Hal, pushing his way through them to the com link on the wall. "We got trouble."

"Hi there Hal." smiled Raan to Hal's back. "I can see you missed us."

"He's right though," Erion sobered quickly, "We do have trouble."

"What's up?" asked Raan, instantly serious.

"Somebody put a bug on the planet hopper."

"What for?" asked Starfire. "And who?"

"That's what I want to find out," Hal looked back with a snarl.

"Surely you can't think it was one of us?" asked Starfire, aghast.

"Well it didn't put itself there. I have to see Tranter and let him know."

"Let me know what?" The object of the discussion had just arrived. All eye's looked in his direction. "What's up, are my pants on fire?"

"It's serious, Tran," began Hal. "Somebody bugged the hopper. One of Thirty Seven's routine checks found it." Tranter spun round, looking at each of them in turn. He stopped at Erion.

"You gave your word My Lady. Do you have any idea what's at stake here?"

"I didn't plant the thing," began Erion.

"Come on Tranter," from Raan,

"Wait a minute, Tran," began Hal. They all began to speak at the same time till Starfire put her fingers to her mouth and whistled loudly. Everyone stopped talking at looked at her.

"Listen, maybe I'm naturally sneaky, I don't know, but when we arrived here, I had Delta Ten do a little checking up. He told me your central computer had sent several encoded messages to someone pretty high up on Auria."

"That's impossible!" said Tranter, shaking his head.

"Look for yourself." countered Starfire defiantly. Tranter didn't answer, but stalked straight through the group and marched purposely towards his office with the rest of them in tow.

"I don't see Jemmi," muttered Raan out of the corner of his mouth to Erion, who had been by his side while they walked.

"I'm on it," she answered, taking one of the tunnels that led to the sleeping quarters. Jemmi was throwing things into a carry-all when Erion walked through the hatch into the girl's room.

"Leaving us?" she asked.

"It's none of your damn business," answered the beautiful woman. She flicked her long hair over one shoulder and zipped up the bag, throwing it onto a table where two others sat ready packed.

"Oh, I think it is my business," began Erion, taking a stepping into the room. "I think you put a transmitter on your hopper, knowing Hal was going to take me to the Cantina."

"That's a lie!" snapped Jemmi.

"I don't think so," said Erion carefully, "I did a lot of thinking on the journey back. The Rebel is Tranter's ship and it's voice operated so you wouldn't be able to get in there to plant a bug on it. When you found out Hal was going to take me to the Cantina, you knew we couldn't use The Rebel for the same reason. You hoped Tranter would give us your hopper. I bet you would have offered it had he not done so."

"You're crazy!" spat Jemmi. "Why would I want to plant a transmitter on my own ship?"

"For the same reason you've been sending messages to Auria," answered Erion.

"I haven't sent any messages. Why would I want to do that?"

"I don't know yet," admitted Erion, "but I aim to find out."

"Get out of my way," Jemmi picked up her bags and made to walk out of the hatch but Erion purposely placed herself in the woman's path."

"Why are you leaving?" asked Erion, "What have you got to hide?"

"Nothing!" gritted the woman. Her bags slid to the floor and she reached in her pocket for a small lady's pistol which she aimed straight at Erion. "I am leaving because I'm sick to death of living on the goddamn ball of steel, and I'm sick of that dammed Aurell and his stupid Alliance. You can have him and welcome to him. Now for the second time, get out of my way." Erion stepped backwards as if to let Jemmi pass, then as she was level with her, Erion lashed out, her straight fingered hand striking Jemmi's gun hand like an axe. Jemmi gave a squeal of pain and dropped the weapon.

"We're going to see Tranter now!" snapped Erion, as she grabbed Jemmi's wrist and forced it half way up her back. Jemmi struggled in vain for a moment, then pulled a matching pistol from her left pocket.

"You're dead!" she spat, twisting and firing in one motion, her beautiful face marred by hate. Erion slipped sideways and down, feeling the hot slice of the beam as it caught her side. She lay on the floor of the cabin, looking up at Jemmi, pain and fear making her feel dizzy as she tried to reach her own holstered gun. As if in a dream, she saw the woman looming up in front of her, the bore of the gun looking as big as a cannon as it centred on her face. Jemmi suddenly crumpled and fell, a deep red stain blossoming across her chest. Tranter stood just inside the hatch, his gun still lined on the fallen girl. He stepped forward and went to his knees beside her, his face pale.

"Why did you do it?" he asked her gently. Jemmi raised a slender hand to touch his cheek but it fell away and her eyes closed as death took her. Tranter sat on the floor, holding the woman's body, not conscious of Raan entering the room to reach down for Erion. She managed to rise with his help and staggered out into the corridor where Hal and Starfire were waiting.

"She had another gun!" blurted Erion, "I should have checked for it. I deserved to be shot!" She fell unconscious into Raan's arms.

"Quick, get her to the medicentre." snapped Starfire, leading the way. She raised her wrist and spoke into her comlink. "Del, meet us at the medicentre, you're going to be needed in your doctor mode. Erion's been shot."

"Understood," he answered. Starfire risked a glance at the unconscious form of Erion, draped across Raan's shoulders. Speed rather than comfort seemed to be of the essence and he was almost running down the metal corridors, leaving little droplets of her blood spattering the floor as he went. Delta Ten was waiting at the hatch to meet them and turned aside to let them pass. Raan rushed in and placed the unconscious girl on a couch, fixing monitor wires to her body as Delta Ten plugged the other end into the computer console, watching the readings intently.

"Come on Star," said Hal. "There's nothing we can do here. Let's go find Tranter; he might need some help too." He pulled her away from the hatch and they walked back to Jemmi's quarters. Tranter had arranged the dead woman on her bunk and covered her with a sheet that could not hide the blood that still seeped through. Of the man himself there was no sign and after a quick glance around the cabin they set off to look for him. He was in his office, standing by the huge opaque screens, gazing out into the void of space. He didn't turn when they entered but raised a hand as if to acknowledge their presence. He looked so forlorn and lost that Starfire's heart went out to him. Shrugging free of Hal's restraining grip, she walked over to him and called his name.

"I killed her," he said simply.

"You had to, Tranter." He shook his head and looked down at the pistol still in his hand. He raised it up and hurled it at the wall where it rebounded with a crash and skidded across the floor to land with a plop in the pool.

"I've known her for two years," he sounded incredulous. "I killed her."

"Stop it," begged Starfire. "You're only hurting yourself."

"Why the hell did you come here?" snarled Tranter, turning fast and glaring at Starfire. She met his gaze without flinching, seeing his fists clench out of the corner of her eye and wondering if he was going to strike her. Then the mad light left his eyes and he raised his hands in defeat. "I'm sorry," he began, "It's not your fault. I checked my com logs. You were right, someone did send signals to Auria. I haven't broken the code yet, but I will. Maybe your smart ass android can help me. Where is he by the way?"

"He's in your medicentre with Erion," answered Starfire.

"God I forgot about her. How bad is she?" He looked down at Starfire and hooked a finger under her chin. "Hey, she'll be alright; she's one tough little soldier." Tranter was beginning to sound like his normal self and Starfire relaxed, allowing a feeble smile to cross her features. Hal walked across the room carrying three drinks. These were accepted and they sat on Tranter's couch, waiting for news of their injured colleague. Long minutes passed in silence until Raan's voice broke in.

"Starfire?" She raised her wrist to answer him through her com-link.

"Raan, how is she?"

"She's lost a lot of blood, but she's going to be okay. Del's pumping a substitute in her and he's cleaned her up. The beam didn't pass through anything vital. Luckily for her Jemmi couldn't get a killing angle that's what saved her." Three glasses raised and clinked together in celebration and Raan's voice could be heard through Starfire's link. "Pour one for me, I'll be right there!" He was true to his word and joined them almost immediately, accepting a drink from Max, the robo butler. The hover trolley had mixed Raan his favourite tipple and held it out to him as he passed by. Raan sipped it with relish and sat down by Starfire with a grateful sigh.

"She's sleeping now," he said. "Del's given her something to knock her out for a bit."

"Get him in here, then," said Tranter. "I want to try and decode these messages."

"There's something else he could do as well," began Hal.

"The General left a data card with Erion. Apparently Delta Ten has some sort of link with the Federation main computers. The information on that card could be something to do with all this."

"Let's get these messages decoded first." Tranter disengaged the computer keyboard from its mounting and sat with it on his lap, logging in. "I want to know if we've been compromised here." A stream of symbols flashed across the screen, accompanied by intermittent bleeps.

"We'll never decipher that," stated Starfire. "It's in some sort of machine code."

"I can see that," retorted Tranter. He stopped the recording and tried again slowing the information down. Delta Ten entered the room at this point and stood in front of the screen, digesting the information.

"Sir," he began at length, "I believe I might be able to help if I can communicate directly with your computer."

"Can you do that?" asked Tranter.

"Of course he can," put in Starfire, who didn't have a clue whether he could or not. "Let him get on with it." The android twisted one of his finger tips and it hinged downwards. A small rod slid forward and he inserted this into the terminal direct input port. A few seconds later he broke the link and turned to face them.

"It appears that the sender has been working for the Federation for at least eight months, supplying information gleaned from you, Mr Tranter. Origin co-ordinates of the so called 'Cantina' was the prime objective and the last message promises a speedy conclusion to that end."

"Jemmi was with me for much longer than that," mused Tranter. He snapped his fingers. "Hey though, she did go on vacation to Auria about eight months ago, I didn't think anything of it at the time but she could have met someone, been blackmailed."

"Or bought," put in Starfire,

"Hell whatever," began Raan. "She didn't get that information from her ship so your secret's safe."

"What have you done with the transmitter?" asked Tranter, turning to Hal.

"It's still on the hopper. We disabled it but it's still attached to the navigation equipment. I wanted to get straight back here."

"After dinner, we'll go take a look at it," said Tranter. "See if we can work out where it came from."

"Sir, if I am no longer needed, I would like to look in on Major Erion." said Delta Ten.

"Tell you what," answered Tranter, "We'll all look in on Erion." She was pale, but smiling, sitting propped up on the medicouch and still attached by wires and tubes to the computer.

"How do you feel?" asked Star fire.

"Better now these things are out of the way," she answered, lifting her arm so that Delta Ten could remove a tube from her wrist. "This plastiskin is great stuff but ooohh it itches."

"Don't scratch!" snapped Raan, batting her hand away.

"Can I get up?" asked Erion, turning large pleading eyes towards the unaffected Delta Ten.

"Only if you rest quietly," he answered. "The wound was deep but the plastiskin has taken well and I don't want it to work loose and become infected."

"I'll be careful." Del pulled back the sheets and she slid her legs over the side of the bunk and stood up carefully. She gazed around at the concerned faces and grinned, "I think I'll be able to manage to dress myself." The hint taken, they waited outside for her to appear, immaculate in a silk trouser suit that drew admiring glances.

"Where did you get that from?" asked Starfire. "It looks like pure Valasian silk."

"From a Valasian Princess called Elkrist." answered Erion. "And don't worry, I have one for you too." She smiled wickedly, "A size bigger of course." Starfire ignored the jibe.

"What Princess? Who's Elkrist?"

"I'll tell you all about it over dinner," said Erion, "I have a proposition to put to you all."

"And we have one to put to you." answered Starfire, thinking about the ship. Max had dinner laid out for them on their return to the big room and they arranged themselves around the central table. The atmosphere was subdued and the cheerful banter that usually abounded during mealtimes was absent. Erion began by describing the people she had met, starting with Thirty Seven and ending with Gant.

"Since the Coup, this whole system is in chaos," began Starfire. "I've been trying to find out what's going on but the Police have taken over the Galaxy News. According to them, General Dubois and Commander Nooran were behind a plot to take over the Federation. This guy Roland is being hailed as the saviour of the Universe. There have been changes at the top of the tree in the Police and the Marines and a lot of officers have been arrested. It doesn't look good for anyone who was loyal to your father, Erion."

"Gant has a lot of information," began Tranter, "But I doubt he'll share it unless you join the Alliance."

"We have to do something," said Raan, "We can't stay here forever."

"What about if we all go over to the Cantina and talk this all out," suggested Raan. "We need to know what's going on out there before we make any sort of decision."

CHAPTER 17

For the second time in less than two days a party from Tranter's base set off for the Cantina. They had decided to buy the new ship and used the opportunity to give a it a try out. Tranter accompanied them and sat with Starfire, Raan and Delta Ten in the crew compartment.

"I like this ship!" exclaimed Starfire. "You could have had us in mind when you built her Tran, she's just what we need." Her fingers danced over the multi coloured glass panels in her console. "She flies like a light bomber but there's enough room in the hold to carry some pretty extensive freight. Six good sized berths and a great crew lounge, gym and a separate diner."

"Will you shut up!" smiled Raan. "You sound like you're trying to sell it."

"I just like this ship," Starfire glared at him. "I'll like it even better when it's re-named."

"Yeah," put in Tranter. "And while we're on the subject, what sort of a name is Grennig? What does it mean?"

"It's not a what, it's a who," explained Starfire. "It's someone we know who always wanted to go into space and isn't going to get the chance."

"At least it's short," grumbled Tranter. "Won't take too long and use too much paint."

"Will you look at that," said Raan, pointing towards the asteroid field.

"Impressive, isn't it?" stated Erion. Tranter spoke into the comlink to identify himself and gave an assurance that the navicom would be disengaged before going further and they entered the field. Tranter knew a more direct path and they approached the planetoid in half the time it had taken Hal and Erion the day before. The crew hatch opened and Erion walked in.

"I like this ship," she announced. "I've picked out my cabin already so hands off number two, everyone."

"Where's Hal?" asked Raan.

"Still in the lounge, better put the lights on through there," said Erion. Starfire hit the landing notification button and seat belt signs lit up in all compartments, accompanied by a little chime. The crew in the pilot section seated themselves and buckled up for the landing.

Gant was waiting for them at the aircar exit and ushered them through the Cantina lounge into Thirty Seven's large office. The dented old robot rose from behind his desk, greeted them all with a low bow and motioned them toward a row of chairs in front of his desk.

"Welcome to my Cantina. I hear from Con Tranter that you wish to learn more about our Alliance."

"We realise it's a big step," began Erion. "and we know there will be no going back if we decide to join."

"The question is," began Thirty Seven, "If you don't join us, what are you going to do? You cannot go back to the Marines and you will need other identities should you wish another form of employment. The Federation is growing bolder every day and we need good people to block their plans."

"I haven't anything better to do," said Starfire.

"Might be exciting," put in Raan. "Count me in."

"I made a promise to my father to carry on his fight. I'm with you." Erion spoke firmly, then she turned to look at Delta Ten, who was standing behind her chair. "Del, as of now you are a free machine, like Thirty Seven. What do you want to do?" The android bowed politely to her.

"I cannot change my basic programming, which is to care for your safety. I should like to remain with you in voluntary service as your science officer." Erion nodded and they all looked at Hal.

"I don't like the way things lie with the Federation, any more than you do but I work better alone."

"It's your life, Hal," said Erion. "You live it how you want."

"We owe you a lift if nothing else," began Starfire, not quite keeping the disappointment out of her voice. We'll take you wherever you want to go."

"Thanks," said Hal, standing up. "My old room free, Thirty Seven?"

"Take it, my friend," answered the tall black robot. "Orlando will give you the key." Hal nodded to the others and walked from the room.

"I just don't understand that guy," said Raan, shaking his head.

"He is a very private man," said Thirty Seven. He looked at them all in turn, saying, "Indeed, you must all be very special people for him to recommend you to us."

"He did that, huh?" mused Raan.

"He said that, even considering you had only just met, you were the tightest small combat force he had seen and we would be foolish not to ask you to join us as a strike team."

"That is what you have in mind for us then, is it?" asked Erion.

"Something along those lines," agreed Thirty Seven. "We are still gathering information at the moment."

"Information!" snapped Erion. "Father left vital information stored with Del. Thirty Seven, may I use your main computer? I'd like Del to hook up with it, please?"

"Of course," he answered, turning to limp back to his desk."

"Hey!" began Tranter, "Do you think your smart ass android could fix up Thirty seven? It must be years since he had an overhaul."

"Ask him yourself," said Erion. "He's a free machine now."

"I would be honoured," stated Del.

"Now," began Thirty Seven, "since you have agreed to join us, please remain in your seats and do not be alarmed." He pressed a button on his desk and the semi circular room slowly moved round. They travelled 180 degrees and the room stopped moving with a soft click.

"Come and meet the others." Thirty Seven rose from his chair and opened the door that would have taken them back into the Cantina Bar. It now opened onto a busy command centre. "There's two offices exactly the same," explained Tranter as he led them past a bank of computers, staffed by smiling Aurians. "When it revolves round, there's a red light over the bar. It means Thirty Seven don't want to be disturbed, so no one will try to get in to see him. If anyone did, all they'd find is an empty office. They'd just think he'd left by the other door." They turned left and went through another set of sliding doors into a large, white room. A raised platform at one end had several chairs on it and the whole wall behind it was comprised of a computer screen. The rest of the room was laid out like a large, open plan office, with several work stations and cubicles. The wall to the right held banks of computer terminals and the wall to the left carried several screens. Some were dark, but others showed views of the Cantina Bar and the launch bays. Gant, Elkrist and the Cloud brothers rose from one of the tables near the raised platform and Gant introduced them all.

"Welcome to the Alliance," said Elkrist. She took Tranter's hand. "I am sorry about Jemmi." Tranter looked down at his feet and nodded his thanks.

"Now," said Gant after they had all been introduced and seated themselves around a couple of tables, "Apparently, General Dubois has sent us some information." Erion delved into her pocket and produced the card. Jed Cloud took it from her, sauntered over to one of the computer stations and inserted it into a slot. The big screen on the far wall immediately lit up with a logo they had not seen before.

"What's that?" asked Erion. They shook their heads. The letters A, F and P were intertwined with two venomous snakes, the whole scene encased in a revolving star map of the Aurian System.

"That's the program loaded," began Gant, his calm eyes searching Erion's face. Where's the data?"

Here," Erion produced the crystal. "Delta Ten has the passwords."

"I believe I am carrying that in my memory banks." said Del, "I know I have the knowledge but I cannot retrieve it."

"Del, listen carefully," said Erion, softly. "My father gave me two trigger words for you. 'Helena May'."

"The information is free." stated Delta Ten seriously. He walked to a console, removed his finger tip and inserted the bare end of his finger into the port for direct input at the front of the computer. After a few seconds, data scrolled across several of the terminal screens, the printer started working and reams of paper started to cascade all over the floor. Gant picked up a few pages and scanned them quickly, obviously impressed with what he saw. He ripped off a few pages and started to hand them round. It was half an hour before anyone spoke again.

"This is amazing," purred Elkrist. "I never realised how high the corruption went."

"These names!" added Erion. "Some of them are highly respected members of the council."

"And they'll all be crawling out of the woodwork," said Raan.

"If we work quickly," began Jeddoh Cloud, "We could send our people to these planets and make this information known."

"It may already be too late for that, Jed," said Gant. "There probably isn't anyone left who can do anything about it. By the looks of things, this coup has been planned for years and nothing has been left to chance." A young man in tech overalls walked over to Thirty Seven, bent low over where his ear would be if he had one and whispered a message. Thirty Seven nodded and the boy left the room.

"It seems," he began, "That Hal has found another contract and has already left with a Merchant Trader who was going to that planet. He told Orlando to tell us that he can be reached through Tamara on Kessell should he be needed."

"He could have said goodbye," muttered Starfire.

"He never does," sighed Elkrist. They all looked at young Buck Cloud, who was rummaging furiously through the mounds of paper scattered all over the floor.

"What's up little brother?" asked Jed.

"That name, 'Tamara'; I've read it here."

"Call it up," suggested Tranter, tapping out the name on the keyboard of the computer. The screen filled with information. It was a personnel file on an Aurian man, living on Kessell. He was a high born and ran the planet wide information and communication services, owning the rights to all the major broadcasting networks on Kessell and its surrounding planets. There were hints of criminal activities and associates on the other side of the law but there were no prosecutions against him. As they read on, it became apparent that the man had bribed or bought his way to the top and a couple of his rivals had mysteriously perished.

"He's one tough cookie," said Starfire. "What does he need Hal for?"

"He's had death threats," pointed out Elkrist. "Perhaps he wants protection. It's Hal's line of work."

"It looks to me like it's everyone else that needs protection from him," said Starfire.

"I believe Hal has worked for this man before," said Thirty Seven. "According to my memory banks, three years ago his young son was kidnapped and held for ransom. Hal was hired to find the child and pay off the kidnappers."

"I can imagine how he did that," muttered Raan.

"Perhaps that's all it is then," suggested Elkrist. "Just another job."

"I don't know," muttered Tranter, running long fingers through his thick dark hair. "There must be some Federation connection. I mean, what's the guy doing in the Federation Computer files if he isn't working for them?"

"Oh, he's on the take, all right," said Raan. "Probably sending out propaganda on the network. Maybe that's all it is."

"Re run it, Tran," suggested Starfire. "Lets go through it again. Maybe there's something we missed. Cross reference it with any information in the Alliance memory banks" They all stared at the screen, carefully reading the names, dates and places associated with the man. Starfire and Erion reached the same conclusion at the same time, gasping and pointing to the information that caught their attention.

"His wife!" snapped Starfire.

"Her maiden name," concluded Erion, There on the screen were the words, 'wife, Orinne Blass'.

"You don't think…" said Raan.

"Check on it!" snapped Erion. Delta Ten rushed to obey her, tapping in the request with fingers that blurred with speed. Starfire hastily filled the others in on Blass's double demise at Hal's hand.

"It is as we suspected," confirmed Delta Ten. Orinne Blass is the sister of the late Dolton Blass."

"He's walking straight into a trap."

"We have to warn him," said Starfire, rising to her feet.

"Easy there, Lieutenant," began Gant, catching her arm. The merchant ship will be in hyperspace now. We won't be able to contact them from here."

"What if we contact Kessell. Leave a message with the port authorities," suggested Raan.

"We will do that," agreed Gant, "I will say I am Hal's brother with an urgent family message. That should tip him off, even if they won't allow me to speak with him."

"That's if they pass a message to him at all, My Lord," said Erion, her worry making her forget and address the man by his title.

"I will find out how Hal was contacted," said Thirty Seven. "It was probably the usual way, which is by coded computer message, but you never know, maybe there will be something we can use." Thirty Seven and Gant left the room and Starfire began to pace up and down.

"There must be something else we can do. Erion, how far is Kessell in real time."

"You can make it in one jump from here. Kessell is a designated stop off."

"Then we can go straight there. We could make it in nine hours," stated Jed Cloud.

"We can't spare you, Jed," said Elkrist. "You have another mission tomorrow. Besides, you are on the number one wanted list in that sector. You wouldn't even get to land before they blasted you away."

"Damn it, El, he's my friend," spluttered Jed.

"He shouldn't have gone off half cocked," mused Cal, the thoughtful one of the Cloud family. "He should have checked his facts."

"He's worked for the man before," pointed out Starfire. "How is he to know the guy is married to Blass's sister?"

"Arguing amongst ourselves won't help Hal," said Erion. "Tranter, can you fuel up our ship. We'll have to owe you the cost."

"We could do a little freighting," suggested Raan eagerly, "I've never worked for a living before."

"Aren't you ever serious?" asked Jed.

"He has obviously not lost anything he loved," stated Elkrist. Three pairs of furious eyes turned in her direction, and Elkrist suddenly realised what Hal meant about them being a tight unit. Somehow, she had overstepped the mark and they had closed ranks against her. She spread her arms outwards as a sign of surrender.

"The Alliance has funds of it's own. We will cover the cost of your refuelling and arrange a cargo for you. We'll have to work out some sort of plan to get you in and out. This planet is in Gant's part of the system. He should be able to help you out with some inside info. Somehow, I don't think his warning is going to reach Hal."

"Neither do I," mused Starfire, "Just you wait till I get my hands on that stupid Terry." Despite the situation, it raised a titter and Gant came back into the room to find them laughing. The look on his face stilled any levity.

"Kessell is under martial law, The Galactic Police are in control."

"We still have to get in there," said Erion.

"You're dead set on going in the new ship?" asked Tranter. He received nods all round.

"Okay then. I can't just paint a new name on her, she'll have to have new identity papers." He motioned to Jed's brothers, lounging by the wall. "You guys give me a hand, will you, I need some strong backs and weak minds."

"Very funny, Tran," grinned Lon, "Just you remember who saved your ass on Rigel Two." They departed, still arguing, meeting Thirty seven on the way in. He informed them he had found out nothing of use. There was just a standard request for Hal to contact Tamara regarding another contract.

"Right then," said Gant, sitting down, "I've been to Kessell. It's a pretty weird place, but there is something that might work." He looked straight at Starfire, "It might be a little dangerous if you're still set on it."

"I owe him my life," said Starfire. "Twice."

"Right then," said Gant, "This is what we'll do."

CHAPTER 18

In the early hours of the following morning, Aurian Standard Time, Elkrist, Gant, Tranter and a gleaming Thirty Seven bid goodbye to the Grennig's crew and watched the corvette lift off to follow its sister ship, Jed Cloud's 'Rising Star', away from the base. Not aware that Delta Ten had memorised their route on the way in, Jed had offered to guide them back out before he set off for his own mission. His brothers, Buck and Callon had already left in another ship for the nearest planet to Kessell to stir up as much trouble as they could, hoping to draw some troops away from the planet. Starfire cleared the asteroid fields and made the jump into hyperspace. Now all they had to do was wait.

"I just hope we're not too late," Raan put into words what they had all been thinking.

"Gant figures this Tamara is a bit of a sadist." said Starfire, "He won't kill Hal outright. He'll want him to stew for a bit."

"That doesn't make me feel any better. Let's just hope that's all he does." said Erion quietly. She had been reading the full dossier on the man and did not like what she had found. If anything, his wife looked even worse, but they just had to hope that Hal was still alive.

"I wish we could have come up with a better plan," said Raan. "I don't like this one at all. There's too much that can go wrong."

"There wasn't the time to think of anything else, Raan," answered Erion.

"Look, I'm the one who's sticking her neck out," pointed out Starfire. "And I say, go ahead."

"You're as mad as she is," muttered Raan.

"Ah, Raan, honey," cooed Erion, "I didn't know you cared."

"Cut it out." he snapped. "I don't think you two realise just what we might be getting into here. A couple of years ago, my unit was sent to a planet in the mining colonies. We stumbled on a slave trading business and shut it down. Starfire, it wasn't pretty. Aurians don't rate the average Terrellian that much, but the Offworlders don't even bother raising contempt. Terrellian are rare, so they're expensive but if you give anyone any trouble on Kessell, they'll sell you off to one of the cheaper outfits that aren't so careful of their merchandise." He had reached out and had taken her hand in his. She squeezed it back, saying,

"Don't be such a mother hen, Raan. I know what it's going to be like but it's the only way we can get landing clearance on Kessell now. This Tamara guy has a house full of Terrellian servants. He must want replacements now and then." She caught his eye and smiled. "Anyway, you said you wanted to work for living. There's good money in the slave trade."

"I don't know why I bother," he sighed, dipping into his flying jacket inside pocket and producing two cigars. "Thirty Seven put me on his list for supplies of these. There's a crate full in the hold. Have one on me."

"Thanks," she answered.

"Now does everyone know what they have to do?" asked Erion. "Starfire you're the luckless Terrellian secretary who unwittingly answered an advertisement for a job with us."

"That turned out to be more than I bargained for," she added.

"Raan, you and I are a couple of High Borns down on their luck who have just turned to the body trade to make a bit of quick cash. That should explain us being a bit raw at this. Del, you are the registered owner of the Grennig. I filed your papers through the Federation computers this morning. Since you are the only one of us without a criminal record, you'll have to do. Now if you're asked, you agreed to bring us here on condition that we pay you when they pay us."

"Erion do you really think they're gonna believe all this crap?" asked Raan, drawing the cigar smoke deep into his lungs and expelling it at her like a dragon.

"I've found that the more unlikely the story, the easier people seem to believe it," she answered, waving away the smoke with a delicate hand.

"We'll find out soon enough anyway," began Starfire. She yawned and stretched. "I'm going to get some sleep. We have nine hours to kill."

Starfire's personal alarm woke her after seven hours and she rose from her bunk for a shower. She emerged from the shower and fluffed out her newly dyed blonde hair. She pulled a silly face in the mirror, then composed herself before walking out of her cabin.

"We're coming out of hyper space." stated Erion. "Stations, please."

"We are in normal space," stated Delta Ten.

"We'll be in communication range in four minutes," said

Erion. "Del, you take the con while we go and get ready."

"This is commercial freighter Grennig requesting permission to land. Do you copy?" Delta Ten was transmitting his request when they re entered the bridge.

"We copy, Grennig. This is Kessell Central Port Authority. What is your cargo?"

"I am carrying food supplies, water and three passengers," answered Delta Ten.

"Permission to land granted. Be aware that Kessell is now under martial law. Please dock at bay fifteen and remain in your ship until a representative of the Port Authority collects you and your passengers."

"Understood, Central," answered Del, cutting the link.

"So far, so good," said Erion, brightly. She and Raan were dressed in expensive robes that had been carefully made to look as though they had seen better days. Starfire wore a smart, pale green trouser suit and a badge that had the name 'Lindi' on it in red stylised writing. Erion had put up Starfire's newly dyed hair in a little bun and decorated it with a red feathers and fake flowers.

"Love the hair," complimented Raan.

"I look like a Bimbo," grumbled Starfire. She looked strangely out of place as she sat in the pilot's chair, landing the big craft in the designated silo. She cut the engines and allowed the big ship to sink down slightly on its hydraulic legs before she stood up and walked towards the hatch, saying, "Right then, let's get this show on the road." She started to walk gracefully towards the hatch, then went over on one heel. She recovered herself without breaking her stride, muttering, "How the hell do women walk in these things?"

"You look just fine to me, precious," Raan winked at her.

"It isn't funny, Raan. I'm a Marine, god dammit!" said Starfire as she tottered towards the hatch. "What if I can't fool 'em."

"Gant told us this Tamara is crazy about Terrellians. He won't be able to resist you."

"Happens to me everywhere I go," sighed Starfire, blowing on her long, false red nails and polishing them on her skimpy jacket. The rear hatch started to open and eight black, shiny jackboots came into view as the hatch rose. Eight grey clad legs were next and, as the door rose higher, the insignia of the Galactic Police could be seen on four huge chests.

"I told you two this wasn't going to work." hissed Raan as the door rose higher.

"No you didn't," hissed Starfire back at him. "What would you do, charge in with guns blazing?"

"Be quiet the pair of you," whispered Erion. "Here we go." They stepped out onto the sloping ramp before it reached the ground and walked cautiously downwards to meet the grey and red clad officers of the Galactic Police. One of them saluted and motioned them to follow. They marched through the bay area, surrounded by the guards and keeping in between the white lines marked on the silo floor. They were deposited outside a large, glass fronted room with a check in desk that ran the length of it. It was sectioned off in several places and people were already there answering questions and handing over computer cards for inspection. Delta Ten was checked in and allowed to leave to supervise the unloading of his cargo. The blank faced man behind their bit of the counter fixed Raan with a smug expression and said.

"Now then, what do we have here? Your papers are a month out of date and this," he motioned to Starfire, "female has none at all."

"We'd like to see someone about her," began Raan, "You see, we kind of came across her."

"They promised me a lift!" gritted Starfire. "Gave me a drink and the next thing I know I'm on their ship, locked in my cabin." She twisted out of Raan's grip. "I demand to see someone in charge. I've been brought here against my will." The clerk looked upon the scene with obvious distaste. He raised the little flap on his part of the desk and signalled two of the guards forward.

"You had better come through here," he said. Raan and Erion grasped and arm each and Starfire was dragged through the gap behind the counter, still protesting loudly. The party walked into an office at the rear of the desks and the clerk spoke to the two guards.

"See that they all remain here." He walked out of the room and silence descended. The guards stood one on each side of the only door in that menacing way that only guards seem to have. There was a desk in the room with chairs in front of it, but they were not invited to sit. Presently, the door opened and an elderly Aurian walked in. He bowed to Raan and Erion.

"Welcome to Kessell. I am Commander Kraith of the Port Authority here. I see you have brought someone who does not have any identification. He leaned forward and peered at Starfire's little badge. "Lindi," he mused. "Pretty name. What do you do, my child?"

"I'm a beauty specialist," said Starfire in a wispy voice. "I must speak to someone. I've been brought here against my will."

"Oh you poor thing," the old man looked crestfallen. "I tell you what. While we are getting this business sorted out, I will send you to one of our most prestigious families. You will be well looked after there at no cost to yourself. How about it?"

"I don't know…" Starfire looked doubtful and the old man patted her hand. "They are fine people and they will welcome you into their home. Don't you worry now. As soon as this business is sorted out you can go home."

"Do you mean it? I can really go home?"

"Of course you can. What sort of place do you think this is?" The old gentleman smiled and patted her hand again.

"All right then, I'll go to these people."

"Very wise." He nodded to one of the huge guards. "Will you find someone to process this young lady through customs and then escort her to the Tamara House?" He waited until a middle aged Aurian woman in office wear popped her head around the door and beckoned Starfire from the room. When she had left, Kraith turned to face Erion and Raan.

"Now then," he began, What are you two trying to prove eh?"

"I don't know what you mean." snarled Raan, eyes looking steadfastly at the floor.

"Come along, young man. We have traced your records, You are Morei and Lowin from the base on Terrell where you work in the administration department. You are supposed to be on holiday. The girl was employed by one of the lifestyle centres there. She took a vacation to visit her brother but she never arrived did she? Because the two of you kidnapped her and brought her here." Kraith glared at the couple. "We do not condone kidnapping. Why did you bring her to Kessell?"

"We thought…" started Erion. "We needed money."

"Did you think we would pay you for this wretched creature?" Kraith looked like he was going to explode and Erion began to think that their plan was not going to work after all.

"Go back to your ship and stay on it till it leaves tomorrow. Do not attempt to enter the city. The Terry female will have to stay here until her immigration papers are sorted out and she has earned her return fare. If you do not wish to end up in the rehabilitation centre, you would be wise not to mention her to anyone. Do you understand?"

"Yes, sir," said Erion quietly. Raan looked up.

"The Captain of the Grennig...."

"What about him?"

"We couldn't pay him," began Raan, not meeting Kraith's eyes. "We thought when you....if you paid us...."

"Get out!" snapped Kraith. Erion and Raan leapt off their chairs and scuttled to the door. When they had left, Kraith looked at his guards, shaking his head sadly. "Amateurs! Go with them. Make sure they go back to their ship." Outside in the corridor, Erion and Raan hurried along, keeping up the pretence in case they were being watched. They rushed back through customs and out into the cargo bays, heading for The Grennig. Not until they were safely aboard their ship did they discuss what had happened.

"That's a good one," began Erion. "Little Lindi will have stay with Tamara until she has earned her fare home."

"That'll be forever then," said Raan. He shook his head in disgust. "It's slavery under another name."

"Well, we have less than twelve hours before our landing permit expires. That should be enough time to get Starfire and Hal back," said Erion.

"I hope Starfire can find him." said Raan. "He'd better be there or we'll have two rescues to do."

There's more than a good chance, I'd say," answered Erion. "According to Gant, Orinne will want her pound of flesh. Hal will be in that house somewhere, if he's still alive. Del, where is Tamara's house from here?"

"It is in the residential district, thirty minutes drive in a hover car," answered the robot.

"We'll have to steal a car." said Raan, "We can't risk renting one."

"What do you mean, 'we'?" began Erion. "If there's any stealing to do, you'll have to do it. I wouldn't know how. I've never done anything dishonest in my life."

"Piece of cake," boasted Raan. He swivelled in his chair to face Delta Ten. "Have you found out anything about the house defences?"

"I have only been able to access the ground floor plans, but it is likely that there will be surveillance devices inside and guards patrolling the grounds."

"I wish we had more time to prepare," said Erion, worriedly. "Has Starfire called in yet?"

"Nothing yet, Major." answered Delta Ten. "She may not be in a position to use the transceiver."

"We'll wait until sundown, then we'll move in." stated Erion. "We'll stick to our plan, such as it is."

"Don't forget Starfire's a Marine. She'll be okay."

"Oh, I know she can take care of herself, Raan. I just hope nobody makes her angry enough to blow her cover."

On the other side of the city, Starfire climbed out of a hover car and stood outside Tamara's Mansion, looking up at the great pink stone building. The door swung silently open and Tamara himself stood there, his hands outstretched in welcome.

"Come in, come in. Kraith has told me about your terrible ordeal." Starfire thanked the woman who had brought her and walked into the hall on the man's arm. "Kraith tells me you are a beautician." Starfire looked down shyly and smiled up at him, hoping that she wasn't overdoing it. "We are having a grand ball tonight so we will have to wait until tomorrow to get to know each other. I know my lovely wife would welcome your expertise." He stroked her arm gently, and Starfire forced herself to smile up at him. "So pale," he murmured. "So soft and pale. Whoops!" he caught her as she tripped and almost fell off her three inch heels.

"Tamara!" called a voice from her left. Starfire leaned past the big man to see Orinne emerge from a side door. Even without seeing the vids of the couple, Starfire would have recognised her. She was as fat as her brother and had the same small, piggy eyes that glittered in her big, round face like orange jewels. She was also under the false impression that crimson satin suited her. She waddled up to him and smirked at Starfire.

"Another new toy, my dear?"

"Please, Orinne. This is our guest, Lindi. She's going to be staying with us until her papers are sorted."

"Really," sniffed Orinne. "Well I'm much too busy to deal with her at the moment. Orinne waved a podgy hand towards a tall, skinny woman, whose faded copper hair was pulled back from her head in a severe bun.

"Marta, please take Lindi to one of the guest rooms and settle her in, would you. Then see me about the menu for tonight."

"Yes, Madam." The skinny woman took Starfire's arm in a vice like grip and steered her towards a curved staircase. As she was being led away, Starfire looked back and saw Orinne and Tamara in conversation.

"How's our guest in the basement doing?" asked the fat woman. "Do you think we have time for more a little more fun before the dinner party starts?" Starfire didn't hear Tamara answer as they were too far away. She was marched to the end of a wide, carpeted corridor at the top of the stairs. They turned right up another flight of narrower stairs and right again along a narrow passage at the top. Marta stopped at a small door and kept her grip on Starfire while she opened it and pushed her inside a tiny room. Starfire was sent sprawling across the floor to land beside a narrow bed in a crumpled heap. By the time she had wrenched off the hated shoes and hauled herself upright, the door was shut and bolted.

CHAPTER 19

"Anything from Starfire yet?" asked Erion.

"It's only been three hours." answered Raan. "Give her time."

"It's just that I can't stand all this waiting around." Erion paced up and down in Grennig's pilot section. "I don't think I'm cut out for all this stealth stuff. I like to know what I'm going to be doing."

"Believe me, something awful will turn up pretty soon and give us a starting point." Raan leaned forward and checked the comlink was still operational out of habit.

"Bimbo to mother hen, come in!" It crackled into life and Raan threw Erion a big grin.

"Star!" called Raan. "Where are you?"

"I'm on the top floor. I'm locked in a pokey little attic room. It has an old fashioned door with a sliding bolt. I'll be out of here in no time." Erion leaned towards the com link.

"Have you found anything out?"

"I think Hal's still alive. I heard Orinne and Tamara talking about a guest in the cellar. I'm pretty sure it's him."

"We're under ship arrest," began Erion. "It will be dark soon so we can sneak out. We should be with you in just over an hour."

"Just be careful. There's going to be some sort of big party here tonight. Lots of VIPs and Police Brass."

"We'll try to get inside and back you up."

"Okay. I'll call you again when I know more. Bimbo out." Starfire broke the link and placed the Lindi brooch back on her tunic. Her little dagger and the hidden transceiver in her brooch had been an integral part of their plans and much had depended on them not being discovered. Starfire took out her laser dagger and quickly sliced through the sliding bolt. The door swung silently inwards and she cautiously poked her head out. The corridor was empty. She broke the heels off her shoes, slipped them back on and made her way down some more very narrow stairs. They emerged in the food preparation room where a harassed chef flitted between several large food dispensers. A swinging door opened and two young giggling Terrellian girls dressed as waitresses walked in pulling hover trolleys. These were loaded with plates of fruit and taken out again. Another door swung open and a tall, snooty looking Aurian entered the room guiding a hover trolley in front of him. This one was loaded to the gunnels with clinking bottles and Starfire guessed the door would lead to the cellars. The waiter spoke briefly to the chef about the menu and surreptitiously handed him a dusty bottle. Starfire watched while the waiter disappeared through the other door and the chef bent down to hide the bottle under a counter. Shoes in hand, she scuttled across the clean white floor and out through the other door. The walls were now bare plastiform, painted cream and the stairs were plain grey. They led down in a gentle spiral and came out into a vaulted chamber. The wall on her right was taken up with racks of wine bottles lying on their sides. Wooden crates filled with beer bottles were piled roof high against the far wall and there was a smaller alcove to the left which was fitted with iron bars. Starfire crept up to it and peered inside. The lighting was poor here but it appeared to contained wine racks also. These bottles and racks were covered in a thick layer of dust and she suspected Tamara kept his special stock here.

"Hal?" she hissed. "Hal, are you there." A low groan reached her ears.

"Hal, stop messing about and answer me."

"Star..." the word came out more like a muffled croak and she stifled a whoop of joy. She carefully scanned the door of the cell but could see no sign of any defence systems.

"I'm going to cut the lock. Standby." she whispered. The power was fading from her knife and It took her five minutes to burn through the bolt. She had to hurriedly hide behind some crates once when the wine waiter reappeared to take more bottles upstairs, then she was through. She slipped inside the small chamber and found Hal standing against the far wall. His wrists were tied to a hook above his head, his black shirt was open and ankles were tied together.

"You look awful." she said. He lifted his head and stared at her, running a dry tongue over cracked lips. Starfire grabbed a bottle from one of the crates, smashed the lid off and dribbled some of the liquid into his mouth.

"Take it easy," she chided, as he gulped down the liquid. "It's beer, not water. He sighed, and tilted his head back against the wall.

"What the hell are you doing here?" he gasped.

"We decided we couldn't function as a tight unit without you," grinned Starfire. Her fingers worked steadily at his bonds, trying to untie the many knots in the cord. "Who tied you up? There must be a dozen knots here."

"That crazy fat woman," said Hal. "I walked into the house and half a dozen guards pulled a guns on me. She brought me down here and had a little fun with me before threatening me with a very nasty end and flouncing off. Between you and me, I don't think she liked me very much."

"That's understandable when you know who she is," said Starfire, untying another knot in the nylon cord. "She's Dolton Blass's sister."

"Oh ho!" said Hal.

"There's something big planned for tonight," said Starfire. "I think you're the star prize." Hal looked serious.

"They don't know who you are, do they?"

"I don't think so. They're so busy with this party they've forgotten all about me."

"Are Raan and Erion here?"

"And Del too." said Starfire. "They're on the outside and I'm on the inside."

"You're all crazy." he muttered. Starfire prodded him with a long finger and he flinched.

"You're not wounded are you?" asked Starfire, concerned. Hal shook his head but she sensed something was wrong and lifted one side of his open black shirt. She winced in sympathy at the mass of bruises and small burns across his body.

"Orinne?" she asked.

"Tamara." answered Hal. "He likes doing; she likes watching."

"I bet he's pretty near the top of your payback list," she said gently, re-fastening the shirt.

"The present favourite," admitted Hal.

"Oh I'm getting nowhere with this," muttered Starfire. She activated her dagger and carefully sliced the remaining cord where it hung over a rusty hook. The strands parted and Hal dropped his arms, feeling the pain of restored circulation as he circled his shoulders and clenched his fingers. Starfire went to work on the cords around his ankles and soon he was free.

"Erion and Raan will be here soon," said Starfire." Hal slid down the wall until he was sitting on the floor.

"Give me a minute." he sighed and stretched his arms out again.

"Sure." answered Starfire. "I'll keep watch." She handed him the bottle of beer again and went to the door to peer out into the cellar.

"Is there another way out of here?" she asked. "The way I came in leads to the galley and then there's stairs to the upper floors at the rear of the house. I'm guessing the other door leads into the dining room."

"That's the way they brought me down here," began Hal. "We've got to get some weapons. That little stick knife of yours won't be enough."

"Apart from smashing a bottle and holding it by the neck end, I can't see anything here that will help."

"Come on," said Hal, rising to his feet with a groan. "We'll no doubt find something. Time to go." He accepted a hand up from Starfire and looked down at her with a grin playing around his mouth.

"What?" she demanded.

"Your hair," He held back a smile with difficulty. "It looks really stupid."

"Frag off!" she shoved him roughly aside and led the way up to the galley.

* * *

"Now that's what you call a house," said Erion in appreciation.

"Yeah," snarled Raan. "Looks like their party is well under way too." Faint strains of dance music filtered out into the night, together with the odd burst of polite laughter. They stood in a small lane at the side of the house, peering over the wall. Twenty minutes later, Starfire called.

"I'm with Hal. He's okay but we have no weapons. We're going to sneak up through the galley to the back stairs and try and find another way out. There's a hell of a lot of activity though. We might get spotted."

"Right. We're going in the front door." said Erion. "We'll back you up if you should need it. Good luck." Erion, Raan and Delta Ten walked round the corner and up the drive to the bottom of a long, wide flight of stone steps. It swept up false, sloping lawns to a large pillared veranda at the front of the house. Two cigar shaped robots hovered at the top of the steps wearing embroidered tabards.

"How do we get past them?" asked Erion.

"Easy," said Raan. "Robot's are stupid. Present company excepted of course." He put an arm around Erion and Del and drew them into a huddle. When they stepped back, Delta Ten walked smartly up the steps while Erion and Raan stayed out of sight.

"Good evening," said Delta Ten politely. The two drones homed in on his position.

"Welcome," began the one on the left. "May I see your invitation?"

"That is what I would like to discuss with you," began Del. "I have lost my invitation, therefore I cannot prove to you that I have been invited. However, I know I have been invited because I was sent an invitation."

"A problem indeed," said the second robot.

"One of you must verify that I am speaking the truth and the other must remain here with me to ensure that I do not gain entry to the house under false pretences."

"That course of action is acceptable," said the first and hummed off to float towards the house. Raan and Erion were already on the veranda, drinks in hand when it passed by them on its way to the entrance hall. They watched it go past and followed it through the huge open doors into the main house.

"I don't think we're going to get Starfire and Hal out of here un-noticed," said Raan, looking at the thirty or so people who milled about the large room making small talk.

"We'll cross that bridge when we get to it," said Erion, helping herself to another drink from a passing waitress.

"There's Tamara," whispered Raan, his mouth close to her ear.

"I see him," she whispered back. "I know that man standing next to him. He's brass in the Galactic Police."

"Will he recognise you?"

"I don't think so. He gave a talk at the academy on crowd control. I was right at the back." She sensed Raan stiffen slightly. "What's wrong?"

"Look what's on the table." Raan motioned with his head. She gasped as she recognised the black gun belt and the huge pistol nestled inside its holster. The rig was arranged on a plinth like a trophy.

"Which way is Starfire?" asked Erion. The sooner we're out of here the better I'll like it."

"East, if Del's map is correct."

"Come on," Erion placed her drink on the table and led Raan onto the dance floor. "Head towards that table." They waltzed gently round in an easterly direction.

"Oh no," muttered Erion. "That old guy Kraith has just walked in."

"Damn it!" hissed Raan. Whatever he was going to say was left unsaid as the galley doors to the kitchen burst open and the chef staggered in backwards with flailing arms and a cleaver sticking out of his chest. He was closely followed by Hal and Starfire, who held large, gleaming knives.

"Hal!" yelled Raan. He scooped the holster from the table and threw it across the room. Hal leapt into the air and caught it, one hand snatching out the pistol and firing at the Galactic Police Commander, who was the first to react and who was already aiming a gun at them. He crumpled and fell against Tamara who also had a gun in his hand, spoiling his aim. Erion and Raan delved under their clothing, brought out hand guns and fired into the air. Guests screamed in terror and milled around in confusion while some dived to the floor and others ran for the exits.

"Tamara!" bellowed Hal. He shot the big man through the chest as he was correcting his aim. His shot missed Hal by inches and hit a hapless guest who slid to the floor.

"No!" screamed Orinne. She picked up her husband's fallen pistol and started to shoot at staff and guests alike in her fury. Raan and Erion both shot her at the same time and she was flung backwards to collide with one of the buffet tables. It collapsed with a crash, adding to the din.

"Come on!" yelled Raan, firing at a robot guard. They made for the hall and main doors beyond, firing at guards as they went. Hal covered them from the veranda as they dashed down the steps, then Raan turned at the bottom to cover Hal as he joined them. "This way!" he motioned with his gun around the corner and they ran into a dark side alley. Raan had disabled the street lighting and their darkened aircar was waiting for them at a side entrance to Tamara's grounds.

"Where's Del?" asked Starfire as she slid into the back with Erion.

"Gone back for the ship." she answered as Raan powered up the car. It rose on a silent cushion of air and headed into the street. Several Galactic Police and a couple of off duty Marines barred their way but Raan headed straight for them. Two were knocked down and Hal wounded another before they shot by them and into the main road.

"They'll have police out looking for us." said Starfire.

"That's why we're not going to the launch bay." said Erion. "We're headed out of the city to meet Del. That we should avoid any patrols."

"What, like that one, you mean?" asked Starfire. An armoured police car squatted in the centre of the road, all of its searchlights pointed in their direction. A wicked little ion cannon was mounted on its roof. That too, was aimed at them. Raan stopped the car.

"Leave the vehicle and come towards the truck with your hands raised or you will be destroyed," a voice boomed from the speakers. "You have twenty seconds to comply. There will be no further warnings."

"We're dead," sighed Raan, flatly.

"I'll try for the Cannon," said Hal softly. He leaned the

muzzle of his blaster on the window sill and took careful aim."

"It's probably shielded," said Erion. Hal ignored her and fired. The armoured vehicle exploded and lifted high into the air, opening out like a flower. It turned slowly over and landed on its roof with another thunderous explosion thirty feet away, scattering burning fuel across the road in a river of fire.

"Fraggin' hell!" exclaimed Starfire. "What is that thing loaded with?" Hal shook his head in disbelief and squinted up the barrel. The starlit sky darkened for a split second as Grennig roared overhead at zero height. It hovered just above the ground in a nearby field, which lit up as Delta Ten switched on the downward pointing landing floods. Smoke still dribbled out of its forward missile launcher and it turned away from them to lower it's aft boarding ramp. Raan powered up the car, turned it towards the ship and crashed through a wooden fence to get into the field. He drove straight up the ramp and into the rear hold, almost hitting the opposite wall. The ramp started to close immediately and they felt the ship rise before it rumbled shut with a metallic clang.

"More police are closing on our position," said Del's voice over the comlink.

"Starfire get us out of there!" ordered Erion.

"I'm on it," she answered, sprinting for the pilot section. "Well done, Del," she gasped as she slid into her chair and snapped on her seat belt. After a brief check on the ship's status, she pushed a control lever all the way forward, lifted the ship's nose high and gunned the rear drive engines to force the little bomber straight up into the sky like a rocket.

"Unorthodox, but effective," he said, peering downwards. "I have not seen this manoeuvre carried out before."

"No, you wouldn't have," she admitted, ignoring the yells

and thuds from behind her in the crew lounge section. "It leaves a great big smoking crater on the ground so it's illegal, it's hard on the engines and even harder on any passengers not strapped in." The rest of the crew staggered up the incline and strapped themselves into their seats with difficulty. "Ignore the seatbelt rule at your peril," she sang. "In flight safety manual rule four, sub section...Ow!" She glared at Raan, who had thumped her arm.

"I damn near broke my neck back there." Raan tried to look angry but couldn't quite keep the admiration from his tone.

"Stop whinging and check for signs of fighter pursuit." said Starfire.

"I am," he said, baffled. "There's nothing. I don't get it."

"Would it have something to do with that big red glow over there do you think?" asked Erion, pointing out of the starboard view port.

"I planted several mines in the Galactic Police launch bay silo before I left," explained Delta Ten. "I thought it might hasten our escape if they were unable to launch their fighters."

"Making you a free machine was the best thing I ever did," said Erion.

"We have orbit confirmed." he answered.

"Fighters on the long range scanners," called Raan.

"How many?" asked Starfire, worriedly.

"Too many for us to deal with," said Erion. "Your course is plotted and laid in, Lieutenant. Get us out of here." Starfire pushed a button and The Grennig shot into hyperspace in a brilliant flash of colours.

CHAPTER 20

"Normal space in ten seconds," stated Delta Ten from his science station.

"Hail Tranter's base as soon as we are out of hyperspace please Raan," ordered Erion. "Get permission to dock." Tranter was waiting to greet them at the entrance hatch.

"Welcome back, man. I thought we'd seen the last of you," said Tranter as he shook Hal's hand.

"No such luck," Starfire brushed past them heading towards Tranter's big lounge. "I'm gonna tell that Max to cook us up a great big four courser. The food on that ship sucks!"

"Everything all right here, Tran?" asked Hal.

"Jed's off somewhere in The Rising Star but it's pretty quiet other than that."

"And how are you?" asked Erion, gently.

"Keeping busy, Major. Just keeping busy." They reached the big room to find Starfire trying to summon the hover trolley.

"Max! Where are you, you stupid appliance?" She turned to Tranter.

"Perhaps it's broken. When's the last time you used it?" Tranter sighed.

"To be honest, I haven't. Kind of lost my appetite."

"Damn it," muttered Starfire. She caught Delta Ten's eye. "Can you cook?"

"Never mind that, Starfire," began Erion. "I have a funny feeling about this. Del, scan for anomalies." It didn't take him long.

"There have been two further coded transmissions to Auria and Jemmi's planet hopper is no longer docked at its station."

"Oh Frag!" Tranter put his head in his hands.

"What is it, Tran?" asked Raan.

"I should have realised," he said. "I've been so stupid! When Jemmi came back from her trip last year, she bought me a present."

"Don't tell me," began Starfire.

"Yeah," he looked up at her. "A robo butler trolley."

"Tran, did you take the transponder out of Jemmi's hopper?"

"Yeah, I did that much. They won't be able to find the Cantina."

"But they know where you are now and about your involvement with the Alliance," said Erion. "You're not safe here."

"What would the Federation want with me?" he asked. "I don't have anything they want."

"You know where the Cantina is," began Hal. And you know all about the Alliance. They'd get it out of you."

"Let's go and see Gant," suggested Tranter. "He always knows what to do." A pleasant little chime emitted from the communications console. "It's the long range scanner," he said, walking towards it. "Fraggin' hell! Looks like three cruisers and a fighter escort." Tranter snapped off the screen. "They're not getting me without a fight."

"Can you get to the asteroid field?" asked Erion.

"Not before they get here," muttered Tranter "He paced up and down in front of the computer consoles, pressing various buttons and setting the station defences. Finally he stood back with a satisfied sigh. "If I don't get back here to disengage the self destruct, this place will blow in sixty minutes. It would not be a good idea to be here when that happens."

"We're with you, pal," Raan clapped him on the back and they made their way to the docking arms.

"See you on the other side." Tranter called out the standard greeting used by pilots before entering hyperspace. He gave them a jaunty wave at the entrance to his tunnel and walked quickly from their sight.

"See you on the other side," murmured Erion. She quickly gathered her wits. "Let's go!"

"Just for once I would like to have a day where I don't get shot at," grumbled Starfire, her hands over the controls doing a very quick pre flight.

"How are we for fuel?" asked Erion.

"We'll have enough for combat," answered Raan. "After that we either drift to the Cantina for a fill up or it won't really matter."

"Understood." she said quietly. "Now, what's the status out there, Del?"

"Three pocket battle cruisers and one fighter escort comprising twelve short range class six Wasp fighters." he answered. "At this rate of convergence, we will be in combat range in six minutes."

"Right," said Erion. "Raan, get Tranter. Let's get some sort of strategy sorted."

"I am picking up communications," said Delta Ten from his computer console.

"Put it on the com," instructed Erion. He turned up the volume for them all to hear.

"This is High Commander Roland, President of the Aurian Council and the Federation Planets. Identify yourselves."

"Con Tranter, Commercial Trader. What do you want?"

"Tranter, I have reason to believe that you have murdered an employee of the Galactic Police and you are harbouring wanted criminals and traitors. I have come to arrest you and take you to Auria for trial."

"I don't know what you're talking about."

"I had hoped you would take that line with me, Tranter." sneered Roland, "Now I can blast you out of the sky with a clear conscience."

"You sound as though you think it's gonna be easy," snarled Tranter.

"You haven't a chance, half breed. Give yourself up, denounce your rebel friends and I might let you live."

"You can go to hell, Roland." Tranter snapped off the link and static filled the pilot section.

"Well that sure told him," muttered Starfire. Now do we play it?"

"There's three battle cruisers out there," murmured Hal, "and twelve short range fighters. I'd say it doesn't really matter how we play it, just as long as we take a load them with us."'

"This is what we like to hear," smiled Raan, "A good inspiring pep talk to cheer us on our way."

"Follow Tranter, Star," ordered Erion. Starfire turned the graceful ship onto a new heading, straight into the path of the three bombers and the fast approaching fighters.

"They'll have The Grennig on their screens now," she warned.

"This is Commander Roland to unidentified ship. State your name and business." They all looked at Erion who made a throat cutting gesture. Static greeted Roland's words and he spoke again. "Unidentified ship, you will answer or prepare to be destroyed." A long ten seconds passed. "Very well, you have made your own choice."

"The fighters are headed this way," called Hal.

"They have to pass Tranter first," said Raan, then, puzzled, "He's letting them through. What's he up to?"

"He has bigger fish to fry," murmured Hal.

"You can't mean those cruisers?" asked Starfire, aghast.

"No!" snapped Erion. She switched on the com link and said urgently, "Tranter, Come in please."

"Erion, don't worry your beautiful head about me. You look after yourself. I'll see you on the other side."

"It's Erion Dubois." yelled Roland. "The Terrellian traitors are on that ship. Destroy it! Kill them all." He was fairly screaming in his anger. Starfire looked across at Erion.

"I think we may have overplayed our hand a little by letting him know who we are."

"Too late now," said Hal flatly as the first of the fighters reached them. He blew it out of the sky and Raan took out another.

"And then there were ten," said Raan coldly.

"Listen!" cut in Starfire, who was still patched in to the communications.

"Tranter," Roland was speaking again. "That girl friend of yours was a Federation agent. She reported everything back to us you know. Everything." Silence greeted his words. "She was very naïve and eager to prove her loyalty; the new recruits always are. She sent us some fine recordings of your, shall we say, intimate moments? They have been greatly appreciated by our troops. I could beam them to your console if you'd like a last memento of her?" A snarl was the only answer and Starfire gasped out.

"No Tranter!" Tranter's ship hurtled forward, straight at the massive cruisers, just out of their own range. The sleek black craft shot like an arrow between the ships, going too fast to be hit by their laser fire. The Rebel exploded as it was midway between two of the cruisers, the star studded black sky erupting in a silent corona. One cruiser was destroyed completely and the other rolled across the heavens to end up drifting in space, it's starboard side rippling with ongoing explosions. The shock wave hit the remaining cruiser, which spun end over end, it's gyros strained beyond breaking point, clipping one of the little fighters and causing it to explode. The cruiser withdrew, listing slightly and moving erratically. If Tranter had been there to hear it, the panic stricken voice that called desperately to his remaining troops would not have made him happy, for it was Roland. The brave pilot had missed the man he wanted to kill the most.

"All fighters regroup and attack that ship. I must be protected. Call in reinforcements."

All but Hal on board Grennig were stunned by Tranter's sacrifice. He was taking advantage of the momentary shock this had caused and picked his way through the remaining fighters. Two more exploded without knowing what hit them in the twelve seconds that it took for space to settle down.

"Shields failing," warned Delta Ten who was calmly at his science station.

"Damn it, where's my heads up?" yelled Starfire as the glowing green symbols disappeared from her view port.

"Guidance system is damaged," Delta Ten might have been talking about the weather. "Repair computers are off line."

"Move it all of you!" snapped Hal."

"You unfeeling Terry," cried Erion. "Tranter was your friend."

"Then don't let his sacrifice be in vain," snarled Hal. His eyes glittered and Erion realised she had wronged the man, but now was not the time for apologies. They were under heavy attack and the ship bucked as Starfire tried to steer it out of the path of the many laser bolts heading straight at them from all directions. Erion looked down at her console and cursed.

"There's another cruiser on the long range scanner."

"For Frag's sake!" muttered Starfire. "Just how bad is this day going to get?"

"One way or another, it'll be over soon, Lieutenant," called Raan from the gunnery section.

"Two fighter's breaking off," called Delta Ten.

"Less for us then," snapped Erion, peering into her navigation grid. "They're headed for Tranter's base." The Grennig lurched suddenly as a fighter exploded in front of them.

"That was almost too close for comfort." called Starfire, wrestling with her controls.

"That wasn't me," said Raan. He looked across at Hal, who shook his head.

"Yowee a fight!" yelled an excitable voice over the air.

"What…who?" gasped Starfire.

"You guys need any help?"

"That cruiser isn't a Federation ship," gasped Erion. "It's

Jed!" She pressed the comlink on and spoke hurriedly into it. "Rising Star this is The Grennig. Can you give us a hand?"

"You got it, kid." yelled Jed Cloud. "Where's Tranter? It's not like him to miss a good fight."

"He bought it," said Hal from his station.

"Oh damn," muttered Jed Cloud softly, then he rallied. "Come on boys, let's go to it," The Rising Star, sister ship to the Grennig and also modified by Tranter, joined in the affray. The battle didn't last long after that. It didn't help once the Federation ships realised who they were fighting as the propaganda put out by the Galactic Police had been explicit and grossly exaggerated. It had also been believed and Jeddoh Cloud and his brothers had been given a terrible reputation. After two more fighters exploded in battle, the remaining ones wasted no time in heading off across heavens after Roland's ship.

"Hal, you there?" It was Jed Cloud.

"Sure."

"How'd Tranter get it?"

"Took out two cruisers with the Rebel."

"Always said that boy had style." A sudden flare on the aft screens caught Starfire's eye. The sky lit up again and Jed shouted. "What the hell was that?"

"Tranter's base," said Erion. "He set it to self destruct."

"Too early," grunted Hal. "They blew it up."

"Man, that's mean," said Raan.

"They didn't do it for meanness," said Hal. "That robo trolley of Tranter's overheard us talking about the information the Colonel left with Del. He must have figured we ran it through Tranter's computers. It's that they wanted to destroy."

"Then there must be something in it we can use against him then," said Starfire.

"I just want to get my hands on that conniving little trolley," muttered Raan.

"I always thought there was something a little too smooth about that robo butler," mused Starfire. "I bet he managed to get to safety."

"We'd better think along those lines ourselves," put in Erion, "before those reinforcements arrive." She caught Delta Ten's eye. "Can you pilot us to the Cantina from here?"

"Of course." He waited for Erion to rise from the co pilot's seat and held out a hand for her to take. The buffeting had taken its toll and she pressed her hand to her side. Raan left his seat and lifted her hand to see blood on her fingers.

"You'd better lie down," he said, supporting her until Delta Ten reached them.

"The plastiskin has come away from your wound," said the stoic robot. "I will take you to the medicentre." Without waiting to see if she wanted to go or not, he scooped her up into his strong arms and marched out of the pilot's section.

"Wait," she ordered, turning to look over his shoulder, "Hal..." she began, wanting to explain her outburst just after Tranter's death.

"Forget it," he growled, not looking up from his station. She didn't pursue the matter and allowed herself to be taken through the hatch. Hal eased himself down beside Starfire and spoke into the comlink.

"Jed, we're going to the Cantina. We're low on fuel. Can you stick with us?"

"Sure. I'll get us clearance. You just follow my tailpipe." called Jed. He gunned his motors and The Rising Star set off across space with Grennig close behind it. Delta Ten returned to the pilot section with the news that he had given Erion something to make her sleep.

"Just as well," mused Starfire. "She was getting pretty close to that crazy scrap man."

"Yeah," agreed Raan. He was a good pan player."

"And a pretty good pilot," admitted Starfire, "That was some stunt he pulled."

"It was typical of Tranter," said Hal quietly. "This time it didn't pay off."

"He was a good friend, wasn't he?" said Starfire gently, not taking her eyes off the screens in front of her.

"I'd known him a long time," admitted Hal. "Roland is a dead man." It was the first time they had ever heard Hal make a threat and Starfire shuddered. Sometimes, she thought to herself, Hal was more like a machine than Delta Ten. Raan stood up, walked to the computer station and asked it for a hard copy of the ship's deck plan. A print out duly arrived and he tore it off, announcing to all that he was going to have a look at the damage below decks, eat a meal and then get some beauty sleep.

"I'll wake you when we get there," promised Starfire.

"Hey!" called Raan to Hal. The Terrellian swivelled in the chair and deftly caught the black cheroot that Raan threw to him. "You're a pretty good shot for a Terry." Hal nearly smiled and put it in his top pocket.

"You're a pretty good shot yourself, for an Aurian."

"If you do not need me here," began Delta Ten. "I would like to begin work on the repair computers. They will be needed when we attempt to restore the damaged linkages on the power converter couplings."

"I have no idea what you're talking about," said Starfire. "I fly 'em. I don't know what makes 'em go." Delta Ten left the pilot section and Hal relaxed slightly. He crossed his long black clad legs up on the console, leaned back and lit a thin black cigar.

He lit another from it and passed it to Starfire, letting a very rare smile cross his features as he gratefully sucked in the smoke and exhaled with a long sigh. He watched the blue cloud waft upwards to spiral into the air purifier for a moment then placed his feet back on the floor.

"Let me take her for a while." He settled himself in the Raan's co pilot seat and flexed his knuckles. Starfire thought, 'I won't ask if he's capable of piloting a class eight bomber. Somehow, I know he is.'

"Okay, you have the con." She carefully put out the half smoked cigar and slid her seat back on its rails. She tilted it back, placed her own crossed ankles on the edge of the console and linked her arms behind her head. "Wake me when we get to there and don't tell Erion."

CHAPTER 21

There was a very subdued gathering in the bar room of the Cantina. Hal led his party to a large table furthest away from the bar. Jed Cloud and his brothers, Lontrey, Callon and Buck sauntered their way through, looking like the four mean gunslingers they were supposed to be from their mugshot holos. Drinks were ordered and carried over to them by a robo waiter carrying a loaded tray. They were joined by Gant and Elkrist and sat stony faced while Erion related the facts of the fight and Tranter's subsequent demise.

"He was a good man," said Gant softly. "He will be missed."

"I propose a toast." began the sultry voiced Elkrist. "To Tranter, wherever he is."

"Well, thanks guys!" said a familiar voice from a side door. Hal, Raan and Jed stood up, guns half drawn, and the remaining mourners sat with a selection of expressions on their faces ranging from amazement to disbelief. Tranter stood leaning on the hatchway entrance, a long drink in his hand.

"How the hell did you get here?" asked Hal, composure returned. Tranter seated himself at the table, seemingly oblivious to the shock he had caused.

"Well I'll tell you. A couple of years ago, I found these two old wrecks, real alien jobs. They'd beat each other up real bad in a fight and there wasn't much left of 'em. They both had something weird on board so I brought them back here and showed Thirty Seven. He figured they were some kind of matter transporter pads so I put one terminal here in the back of Thirty Seven's office and put the other one on The Rebel. Tried it out using booma fruit, but that was as far as it went. Anyway, when I decided to take out those cruisers I figured I'd be dead anyway so I had nothing to lose. I set my ship to blow and activated the transporter two seconds before."

"Why the hell didn't you let us know?" demanded Erion. "All this time we've been thinking you were dead."

"That was my decision, Erion," stated Thirty Seven at Tranter's side. "Tranter activated the terminal and came through but he was almost dead when he arrived. The technology was configured for a non human and he was gravely ill. I put him on life support and I decided not tell anyone about him in case he did not survive. I did not want to raise hopes, only for them to be dashed again."

"Well, you're here now," grinned Jed. "You crafty space dog! How many more lives have you got left?"

"What will you do now?" asked Elkrist. "Roland blew up your base."

"So I heard." he answered. "I'm setting up in business here in the rocks. There's another hollowed out asteroid like this one not too far away from here. I'm going to clear a path through and start again."

"You're welcome to stay with us if you want," said Erion, "Not that I know where we're going."

"Or you can come in with us," grinned Jed Cloud.

"Thanks for the offer, guys, but I'll stick with what I know and that's the scrap spacer business. The way you lot fight, you're going to need an emergency repair station."

"Thanks for the vote of confidence," said Raan.

"We haven't done too badly so far," put in Starfire.

"You're on your second ship in less than a month," retorted Tranter. "And this one is combat damaged."

"You can use our limited facilities until you can start your own operations again." said Thirty Seven. He tilted his head in Erion's direction. "The Alliance will fund the repairs to your ship as they were incurred on our behalf." This drew admiring glances from The Grennig's crew.

"Also, we have a mission for you and you'll need a fully functioning ship." put in Gant. He turned to Hal. "You would be needed on this mission." Hal stared into his drink for a moment, then met Gant's gaze.

"Sure. I owe them a debt. They came for me on Kessell. I owe them this one."

"You might have to think again about working alone now." began Gant. "The price Dolton Blass put on your head has been doubled to One Hundred thousand Credits." He looked at all of them in turn, "As it has for all of you."

"It's nice to be wanted," sighed Raan.

"Welcome to the club," grinned Elkrist.

"Well," began Starfire to Hal, "Are you with us or not?" Hal thought for a long minute.

"I guess so," he answered with a weary sigh.

Good," began Gant. "We've reserved a suite for you all on the lower levels. It's pretty basic I'm afraid, but it's no worse than you'd have on your ship. Have a meal, freshen up and we'll meet to discuss the mission in Thirty Seven's office at say, sixteen hundred?" He rose from the table and would have left, but was interrupted by a call on his wrist link. He moved away from the others and placed his left wrist to his right ear and frowned in an effort to hear what was being said above the sounds in the Cantina. He returned to the group and said, "A routine scan has picked up another transceiver emanating from this position. Raan slammed his beer glass down in disgust and Starfire said,

"For Frag's sake!"

"Not again!" gasped Erion.

"You appear to be the source," said Gant, pointing a finger towards Starfire. Two tough looking young men appeared at the table and, although they were dressed in casuals, it was obvious by their stance that they were security of some kind. "Would you please go with these two men?"

"This is ridiculous," said Erion. After everything we've been through, do you think we could still be traitors?"

"It's all right, Major. I'll go with them. I haven't anything to hide." Starfire left with Thirty Seven and the two young men.

She returned fifteen minutes later twirling a tiny silver sphere between finger and thumb. "The medic just took this out of my arm," she said. "When we were on Kessell I was processed through customs. I had to have a medical and they gave me a pretty hefty shot. Hurt like hell too." She rubbed her arm. "Seems they planted a bug in my bicep.

"The signals cannot leave here because of the magnetic fields, but we haven't deactivated it yet," said Thirty Seven. "Starfire had an idea."

***

Three parsecs and four days later, a Federation strike force landed on a high plateau above the jungle on a remote, windswept planet. It was dark, cold and raining. High Commander Roland stood with his Commissioner of Police, Rimek, looking at the scene in front of them with bored indifference. They were watching a team slowly close in on a small, gaily wrapped parcel sitting on a flat rocky plinth. The tableau was lit from above by powerful yellow lights, which showed up the rain in waves as it lashed down. A young captain dashed up to them and saluted, smartly.

"The signal definitely emanates from the box, Sir. Our scanners can not pick up anything, but may I respectfully suggest you withdraw." Roland sighed heavily and pulled up the collar of his black, shiny cape.

"I am cold and wet, Captain. May I respectfully suggest that you send in your drones and open the damn box?"

"Yes sir!" The young man turned and sprinted away into the orange gloom, pointing and shouting orders as he went. Roland turned to his second in command.

"I hope I have not misplaced my faith in you, Rimek. May I remind you that I had Hal and Starfire in my grasp on Kessell and could probably have taken the Dubois woman and Captain Raan as well? If you do not want to end your days as a robo butler, you had better pray that we are wrong as to the signal here. Roland gazed up at the two and a half metre high black robot with disdain. It looked exactly like Thirty Seven, but when it spoke, it's metallic, monotone voice droned on without inflection and would have immediately been identified as Max the Robo Butler.

"While I was at Con Tranter's base I learned that this new Alliance could cause setbacks to our plans. The Rebels and their base must be destroyed. The advantage that we would have gained by killing the traitors on this ship Grennig was far outweighed by the possibility of obtaining the Cantina's co-ordinates."

Roland stroked his long, beaded moustaches.

"The trouble with you Rimek is that you can only think logically," he said. "What makes perfect sense to you would be incomprehensible to an Aurian. "Of course the Grennig crew is nothing compared with the destruction of the Cantina, but we have a saying on Auria; 'It is better to have one wanga on your plate than two in the woods.' And yes, I know I you don't understand what it means, Rimek, which is the point I am trying to make."

"Sir!" called the eager young Captain, "We are about to send in the drone."

"Do it, then," snapped Roland. "Come on Rimek, we'll go behind this rock just in case." The little drone was spherical, about a metre high and covered with various arms and appendages. It hovered forward, buffeted slightly by the wind, and stopped at the parcel. It looked a sorry sight as it sat on the rock. The bright red ribbons were saturated and hung limply over the sides and the wrapping paper was torn and sagging. The robot extended an arm and pulled slightly at it. There was a muffled report and bits of tinsel and streamers cascaded into the air to the accompaniment of party hooters. The little robot backed off quickly and almost overbalanced, rising to wobble back to the waiting captain.

"Look!" Rimek pointed skyward. A little parachute blew towards them, carried by the high winds. Underneath it was a small box. One of the troopers caught it and hurried towards Roland with it in his hands.

"The signal emanates from here, Sir," he said breathlessly. Shall I open it?"

"Go round the other side," ordered Roland. "Open it there."

"Very well, Commander." He disappeared behind the boulder and returned with the little silver ball in his hand. "There was a note, Sir," he began, holding it out. "It is addressed to you." Roland snatched the paper. There were five words on it, each written in a different hand. He read aloud.

"Roland, better luck next time!"

THE END

Printed in the United States
47268LVS00006BA/335